Lesbians Rock

Women Loving Women Volume 1

Ann Patterson

Ann Patterson

ISBN: 0615910610
ISBN-13: 978-061510611

Lesbians Rock

Women Loving Women Volume 1

Ann Patterson

aka. best4writing

Portland, Oregon

Table of Contents

Ann Patterson

LESBIAN LOVING

Looking deep into her eyes

Her longing draws me in

She touches my cheek

I smile at her gentleness

Her lips touch mine

I taste her breath

Our breasts gently touch

Hearts beat in unison

Hands move softly

Our tongues dancing

Clothing drops away

Arms envelop lovers

Insides tremble

Sensations soar

Reaching into love

Soaring in flight

Dedicated to Molly Ann Kretz, my beloved partner

since the year 2000, a wonderful woman I met

after I came out as a lesbian

at age sixty

Part One

Some Doors Close; Some Open

Chapter One

Jane leaned over the bed to kiss Marilyn's forehead. "I love you. I always will." She didn't know if Marilyn could hear her or was aware of anything happening around her.

The hospital room was filled with monitors and machines clicking, beeping, and flashing lights. The nurses and technicians stepped in occasionally to gather information, change something or add information to the computer. None of them spoke to Jane; they allowed her the privacy she needed as she watched her beloved Marilyn in her final hours.

Jane kissed Marilyn's thin, wrinkled hand and held it to her lips as she buried her head against Marilyn's side. Her tears flowed as quietly as Marilyn's breathing was becoming slower.

Jane dozed off to sleep. She had been awake most of the recent forty-eight hours, from the time she had arrived at the Emergency Room, and then waited during testing to determine the extent of damage the attack had caused to Marilyn's heart.

After so many hours of being pushed and pulled from hope to despair, she was exhausted.

Jane found herself in a dream. She was walking in a garden reminiscent of her grandmother's garden in Midwest, Oklahoma. Pushing the branches of the blackberry out of her way, she looked over the rows of turnips, tomato plants filled with luscious red fruit, the okra pods turning yellow at the top of each plant; then she saw her grandmother's print dress blowing in the cool Oklahoma breeze. She was picking green beans and putting one handful after another into the white enamel bucket with the red strip around the rim.

Jane smiled as she remembered her grandmother's preference for bright white enamel buckets instead of galvanized aluminum buckets or pans. So many times, she said, "If it's white, it's clean. You can never tell if those metal things are clean enough for food."

She walked down the space between rows of beets and turnips toward her grandmother.

As she came near, she called out in a soft voice, "Gran, it's Jane. Would you like for me to help you?"

Her grandmother stood up, put her hand on her hip and stretched her back. "Hi Sweetie, I didn't expect you here today." She groaned with pain from her back. "Yes, I would appreciate your help. My back's hurting more than usual today but I have to get these beans picked before they grow tough and become next year's seed."

She reached her arms to share a hug with Jane.

"I've missed you, Gran. You've been gone so long. I never thought I'd see you again; much less find you in your garden picking beans. I remember when I was a little girl and you taught me how to know when they were just right for picking. You taught me so many things when I was a girl."

"Yes, Jane darling, you were always so sweet, and anxious to learn what I enjoyed teaching you. You've been crying. Honey, what's wrong? Your tears are dropping onto the beans and your hands."

Gran stood up and stretched her back again while looking at Jane for her answer.

"I'm not sure, Gran. I've lost something and can't find it. I've been looking everywhere but can't find what I'm looking for. Now I'm in your garden. I'm feeling very sad, but don't know why. I can't remember what I lost, so how can I find it?" She put a handful of beans into the white enamel bucket.

The sun was warm, but not seething hot or laden with the Oklahoma moisture usually making the humidity unbearable. Gran removed the long-sleeved chambray shirt she was wearing. "It's warmer today than it's been all week." She laid the shirt on the ground and continued to fill the white bucket with fresh beans.

Jane smiled when Gran began to sing a hymn. "Lord, plant my feet on higher ground. Lord, lift me up and I shall stand, my faith on Heaven's tableland, a higher plane now I have found, Lord, plant my feet on higher ground."

Jane sang softly with her grandmother while picking green beans to be canned in Mason jars, and put in the underground cellar for a winter day when fresh green beans were not available. She kept trying to remember what she had lost that made her sad, and her eyes kept filling with tears.

When they got to the end of the row of beans, Gran picked up the bucket, put her arm around Jane's shoulders, and they walked back down the rows of beans, past the blackberries and across the driveway to the back porch. Gran sat in her favorite chair and began to snap the beans. She snapped each end of the green bean off, then snapped the bean into several uniform sizes; having done that for eighty years, it was natural for all the beans to be the same size, an inch and a half long.

Jane watched her grandmother. "Gran, you always look so relaxed when you're snapping beans or peeling apples or shelling peas. I wish I could relax that way. Maybe then I could understand all the sadness I'm feeling inside." She moved the antique family chair, handmade with a leather seat, near her grandmother, sat down and snapped green beans.

"Honey," spoke Gran, "What does it feel like?" In her wisdom and life experiences, she knew there was a different kind of sadness for various happenings in a life.

"Well, I feel like a pregnant woman must feel; it's like there's something big inside of me; it's filled my insides, really hard-like. It's as if I'm going to explode if I think about it. If I could just open my mouth and throw up, maybe it would go away, and I'd be fine. But Gran, it seems to stick in my throat so it scares me. Something's wrong, but I don't know what." Jane put her hand on her stomach then her chest. "It's suffocating."

The two of them snapped beans in a rhythm, first Gran then Jane over and over, "click, click, click." Moments later a handful of beans would land in the white enamel dishpan with a navy blue strip around the rim, "clink, clink, clink." The sounds muffled as the pan became full.

"Honey," Gran looked at her granddaughter. It was as if she was watching a child, not a woman of fifty, sitting beside her. "I remember that feeling inside me when I was sitting at my mother's bedside. The doctor said she might be gone by morning and I was so very sad. Whatever was stuck inside me didn't leave until my dear mother breathed her last. But something sweet happened before she did. I was looking at her face and she smiled, then she said something. I didn't understand so I asked her, "What, Mother?" Her answer was strange. She told me "Hush, Corrie, I'm talking to your father." I watched her mumbling words I didn't understand; then she smiled, and took her last breath. Jane, when she found her peace and I knew she was with Daddy, that chunk of sadness wilted away. I know it's strange; but it happened just that way?"

She picked up the dishpan of beans and went to the kitchen.

Jane sat alone in the leather-bottom chair. Tears dropped from her eyes again. She tried to remember what might be making her feel the belly full of sadness. Nothing came to mind. Her parents were both dead and she had no children. She had married once, but it only lasted two years before the divorce. Her recollection of the divorce never made her sad. She got up and went to the kitchen where her grandmother was filling Mason jars with the green beans.

Jane watched her. First she washed the beans, a handful at a time, then she put them into the jars. Then she took a wooden spoon and packed them tightly in the jar. Jane started helping her fill the quart jars.

After Gran set the jars in her pressure cooker and put it on the stove to allow the filled jars of beans to cook, she told Jane, "I'm going to gather eggs and feed the chickens. Perhaps you can watch the dial on the cooker and lower the burner when it reaches fifteen pounds of pressure. You've done that for me many times."

"Sure, Gran." Jane watched her grandmother pick up her egg basket and leave the kitchen.

In that moment, Jane awakened. She looked around and saw she was sitting beside her beloved wife who was dying. Her dream with her grandmother hadn't left her mind as she put her hand on Marilyn's cheek and looked at her face. Jane realized her sweet Marilyn had died while she dreamed.

"What was it Gran said? 'That the body full of pressure against her insides had subsided when her mother died.' Jane realized the same was true for her; the load of sadness was gone.

Her precious sweet Marilyn was no longer suffering. She was now at peace. Maybe she was somewhere with her own grandmother where she would wait for Jane to join her. That was a nice picture, thought Jane; as she closed her eyes letting the tears fall, and remembering how nice it was to be with Gran. She pictured her beloved Marilyn helping Gran finish canning the beans and taking the jars to the cellar as she would have done if the dream had been real.

Chapter Two

Silvia Canfield sat at her desk and turned her computer on. She was on the verge of making a decision far different than she had ever made before; it would change almost everything about her life.

A mother of three grown children, Silvia went to her email account where she read emails from her son and two daughters. All three of them lived in different states; none had settled in Idaho where Silvia had raised them as a single mom. Her son was in the U.S. Marine Corps and stationed in Southern California, one daughter had married a member of the U.S. Air Force then settled in his home-state of Georgia after he had served his four years; and the other daughter lived in Seattle, now a single mom to one daughter. Silvia was considering a move to Portland, Oregon.

Silvia typed a few words in the search box on Google, "Portland, Oregon, gays, lesbians" then clicked "search". Soon there were many sources of information about Portland's homosexual community. She scanned the listings and clicked on "bars", then "Drag Shows" and read about the nightspots in Portland where she could join with those whom she knew had hearts like hers.

While reading about Portland during the next two hours, she thought about her life of fifty-six years. She grew up during World War II in Arizona at a time when nobody spoke the word "homosexual" even though everyone knew about people who coupled with others of their same gender. As a young girl, she never heard the word; on the other hand, she often heard the word, "tomboy," because her parents, grandparents and others said Silvia was one. To her, it simply meant she enjoyed being outdoors instead of indoors. She preferred to let her sister do the indoor chores as they grew up. She helped milk the cows, mow the lawn and carry wood, anything that allowed her to be outdoors.

During her adolescent years in junior high and high school, Silvia played girls' sports. Her favorite was softball with basketball a close second. She was an excellent player and enjoyed a major role on her school's extra-mural teams. During those same years, her sister always had boyfriends, many to choose from. She was with one boy a bit longer than was wise, so ended up with what they called "a shotgun wedding" because she was three months pregnant the day she got married. The marriage lasted long enough for her to have three babies, and become a divorced woman left to raise three children without a father's participation.

Silvia stayed single until after graduating from college, then married the guy who had pursued her during her college years after he completed four years in Uncle Sam's Navy. Silvia was the first person to admit the fact that her "love" for the man was her "appreciation" for his continued interest in her, even when she brushed him off for three years. The marriage took place two weeks after her college graduation; it meant she wouldn't be moving back with her parents after college.

Years later, she was writing the addresses of two of Portland's gay bars in her little notebook. Then she sat back in the chair to think about her heart and her decision to "come out" so late in life. She was no longer responsible for anyone except herself and it would be easy, with her talents and skills, to find a job in Portland. She had worked for the State long enough to ensure a retirement check when she turned sixty-two or sixty-five; and she had a nice retirement savings, so there was nothing to worry about in terms of income.

What was important to Silvia was her heart. She sat at the computer and began to write about the girls and women for whom she had romantic feelings during the years of her life. There was Anne in fifth grade, her best friend until she became her brother's girlfriend. She met Nancy in eighth grade and Evelyn in her sophomore year who became the same brother's sweetheart and wife. The one she pined for the most was Barbara in twelfth grade; the romantic love for Barbara had never left her heart for almost forty years. Even when Lucille won her heart during her thirties, Silvia loved Barbara the most.

She giggled as she was writing about all the girls of her heart during her life. Every one of them had married a man and disappeared off Silvia's radar.

There had never been a time during her life until in her fifties, that she knew she was ready to live the rest of her life as a lesbian. Her children had been most important to her before; but not now.

It was time to live who she was. Even if she never fell in love again, she knew she wanted to be among other women, gay men too, who would understand the conflict she had dealt with all of her years. Nobody else would or could understand, except another homosexual person whose own heart had tugged at them from early life, not having romantic feelings toward the opposite gender; yet living as if they actually did.

Silvia sat at her computer until midnight writing the stories of her romantic heart. It served her as if it was a therapy assignment by her counselor, even though the counselor she went to during her thirties had never suggested such an assignment.

Writing about the girls of her life-long feelings, brought wonderful memories with the girls and women, and gave her many reasons to smile.

The following Friday afternoon, Silvia drove to Portland.

It was a leisurely drive, a clear day, crisp autumn weather with a moderate level of traffic on the freeway. She had been to Portland a few times, not to meet homosexuals, but to shop, so she knew where the Broadway Tavern was located. She arrived there just after five o'clock. It was filled with people whom Silvia assumed were all or mostly gay men and lesbians. She sat at a small table, ordered a hamburger and a coke. The young man who waited on her was friendly and answered various questions about the Tavern.

After eating her hamburger, Silvia was glad when two ladies came in, looked around for a table, and then asked if they could join her.

"Glad to have you." They introduced themselves as Karen and Neva and told her they both worked at the U.S. Bank across the street.

Silvia was glad to no longer be sitting alone. "The crowd here seems so young. I realize it's Happy Hour, people coming from work, but there are so few older than their forties. Where are the older folks?"

Karen, in her thirties, wearing a blue women's business suit, her hair in the newest short style, ordered drinks for herself and Neva, then leaned forward on her arms. "One word, AIDS. Too many of a generation died during the 1981 epidemic. They had the HIV virus before it was even discovered by the researchers. Because it took the Ronald Reagan Presidency so long to acknowledge the need for funding research to find the cause and medications for that horrible illness, too many died. Every person in the room now, lost a friend or lover, or knows someone still waiting for life-saving research to heal or prevent HIV; some are still progressing from the virus to full-blown AIDS."

Neva paid for their drinks, sipped from her glass, then added, "Karen's right. A generation of Americans, and other people across the world, died, or continue to suffer from HIV or AIDS. My cousin, a bright young man with a future, who would have been successful, lasted such a short time after he first got sick. His partner never got it and still lives. That epidemic spread so fast, nobody could predict who would get it; and if you got the virus, there was no stopping you from getting AIDS and death. Thank God, my aunt and uncle loved their son enough to let him be at home so they could provide whatever medical care was available. Nothing could reverse the disease. They loved their son, cared for him at whatever expense, and didn't discriminate against his partner."

"That's good to hear," Silvia said. "I have a cousin who's the source of family whispers. His parents bought a small café just for him and his partner to have a source of income. I knew him as a kid, but saw him only once at a family gathering. That part of me who has always known I'm gay, led me to spend quite a bit of time with Jim that day. On the other hand, the rest of the family ignored him. He didn't join in like everyone else did in family interactions; just kept himself outside the group, any group. We chatted but the matter of being gay never came up. If I had been out back then, I would have spent more time with him. His partner had died of AIDS before he did; I know that was hard on him."

After they finished their drinks, Karen and Neva excused themselves and left the bar.

A few minutes later, three other women came in and sat with Silvia. They introduced themselves to her as Tina, Joy and Marti. She enjoyed their laughter as they told highlights of their day at work.

When they left, a woman Silvia's age joined her. "Hi. I'm Rachel. My, what a popular place this is tonight." She looked around for the waiter, caught his eye and waited for him to come to the table. "I'll take a gin and tonic, and bring another for her."

"Thank you. I'm Silvia." She fluffed her brunette curls and pulled one curl, mostly silver, down on her forehead. "I drove over from Boise today."

"Glad you're here, Silvia. Are you 'out' in Boise?" Rachel smiled and leaned toward her. "I always like to meet new people who come here."

Apparently in response to Silvia's attention to her hair, Rachel used both hands to sweep her short blond waves back over her ears.

"No, I'm not 'out' anywhere except in my own heart. I've spent my whole life realizing something different about me, but today is the first time I've walked into a gay bar or purposely joined a gay crowd. In Boise, I never went to the Gay Pride Parade because I stupidly was afraid someone I knew, might see me there, and might think I was gay. Now, I feel ashamed about that. Today, for the first time in my life, I'm ready to say I'm a lesbian and I don't want to ever be afraid to acknowledge it again."

Rachael reached her hand to shake Silvia's. "Welcome, my friend, to this wonderful community and family. You don't ever need to feel alone or as an outcast here. Silvia, knowing you've found your freedom to be who you are, makes me very happy for you."

She shook Rachael's hand. "Thank you. I've talked to several people here today and let them assume I've always been 'out', but I decided to be fully honest with you, Rachael. I haven't told my family or friends at work yet. But I will. Just being here today has given me a new level of courage."

Rachael sipped her drink then holding it near her lips, talked over the glass. "Continue to be wise, my new friend. Idaho isn't the best place to be 'out' when there could be troubles where you work. Private companies are worse than government workplaces when it comes to practicing discrimination; yet even there, some supervisors find ways to get rid of anyone who might be gay. I've learned that from friends." She looked into Silvia's blue eyes and smiled.

"You're right, Rachel. What I intend to do, is have a job lined up here in Portland, before I 'come out' in Boise. A bit of defensive planning, I think, just might be wise. I've already sent my application for a few openings here in Portland. The Internet is so helpful these days when considering a major move in your life."

Silvia sat back in her chair and crossed her legs. "I've always had plenty of confidence in decision making."

Rachael grinned as she saw Silvia's slender legs. "Are you staying for the Drag Show tonight?" She watched Silvia scratch her knee and smiled.

"Actually, that's why I came here. When I was searching for a gay bar on the Internet, I found two that had Drag Shows. This one and the Rainbow. I've never seen a Drag Queen up close, just pictures, so thought a show might be interesting and fun." Silvia laughed. "Will I be disappointed?"

"Of course you won't. They're wonderful guys who enjoy performing. I know two of the guys who have college degrees in the performing arts. Others enjoyed high school drama productions. Some just love music and dancing, so become Drag Queens. People who don't know a Drag Queen, especially newcomers, think they're some kind of weird. They're not. And, some of them are women dressed in glamorous costumes." Rachel laughed. "Some are comics; most are great dancers who are skilled at lip-syncing the songs."

The crowd in the Tavern thinned out by eight that evening.

Silvia observed the people around her. Those who sat at the bar sharing conversation with the owner, appeared to be a clique of friends; whereas, those who sat at various tables around the room were more open to others.

She noticed one other woman like herself who never left the table, but enjoyed others, as individuals or couples who dropped by, ordered a drink, chatted a while, then moved on.

She found herself trying to predict who would stay, who would leave the bar, which would move to chat with someone else. "People watching" was always something Silvia enjoyed.

The background music was pleasant.

After their drinks were finished, Rachael suggested, "Let's move to a table down there. It's a great place to be when the show starts.

She picked up her tan purse and led the way to the tall table near the stage. Her larger-than-usual gold earrings dangled as she walked.

A young guy stopped at their table. "Hi Rachael. Glad you're here tonight. I'll be the emcee and it's always good to have you nearby."

"Hey, Daniel. Meet Silvia from Boise."

"Hi, Silvia. I hope you like the show." Daniel was young and handsome with his blond hair and soft complexion. As she smiled at him, Silvia wondered if he was old enough to shave.

"Glad to meet you, Daniel."

"Have you been to a Drag Show in Boise? I performed at the Emerald Club last year." Daniel hung the long blue gown he was carrying on a clothes hanger, on the back of his chair.

"No, this will be my first Drag Show tonight." She looked closely at the bright blue gown with rhinestones all over it. "Oh, Daniel, that's gorgeous. Are you wearing it tonight?"

Daniel laughed. "I thought you'd never guess. I'll see you two later; I've got to get dressed and see who my performers are for the show." He took his gown and hurried behind the stage.

While Silvia and Rachael sipped their drinks and chatted, the Tavern filled up again.

Silvia noticed many male-female couples filling the tables in front of the stage. "Rachael, I thought this was a gay bar, but there seem to be a lot of straight couples coming in now. Why's that?"

"Oh," laughed Rachael. "There'll be more straights in here for the Drag Show and in the Disco Room behind that wall, than there'll be gays. We call them 'breeders' since there could be no gays and lesbians if it weren't for the straights having babies."

Silvia laughed with Rachael. "I'd never thought of that before but you're right."

"Oh, yes. Straights love to bring their friends here. And, we're glad they spend their money here; it keeps the Tavern in business. Sometimes, we don't want them here if they come to cause trouble, fights and the like, requiring the police to show up. Otherwise, we welcome them." Rachael saw a couple of women coming her way. She waved at them and they stopped to join the table. "Silvia, meet Nancy and Bertie. Good friends of mine."

Silvia exchanged greetings with Nancy and Bertie just as the background music died away and the room was filled with a loud, fast popular song.

The emcee appeared dressed in a long, sparkly blue gown. "Welcome to the Tavern. I'm Bolivia and am "Here to Entertain You." Lip-syncing the song she danced around the stage.

The audience clapped along to the music and some of them went to the stage to offer a dollar tip to Bolivia.

Sylvia loved watching so many wonderful things happening all at once. During the Drag Show, she counted nine different Drag Queens who performed with high energy, wore beautiful costumes with big colorful wigs and kept the audience involved as part of the ambiance. She was having the "time of her life" with her new friends and the show. She even went forward and gave Bolivia a dollar tip; then was embarrassed that Bolivia kissed her to say, "Thanks."

When the Drag Show ended, Silvia told Nancy and Bertie goodnight, then Rachael walked with her out of the Tavern to her car.

"Silvia, are you staying in town tonight? I hope you're not driving back to Boise."

"No, I'll stay in town until after the Saturday night show. I have a room at a motel nearby. Maybe I'll see you tomorrow." She hoped Rachael wasn't going to invite her to go home with her; she wasn't ready for that, not yet anyway.

"Okay, I'll see you then. I'll be here at noon in case you decide to come early tomorrow." Rachel held the door for Silvia to get into the car, then closed the door and leaned in for a good night kiss.

Before Silvia realized what was happening, Rachel kissed her soft red lips. She smiled because she enjoyed the sensations that swept through her. Her first lesbian kiss and it was nice. "Good night. See you tomorrow, Rachel."

Silvia awoke by eleven, showered and dressed in tan slacks and a red long-sleeved blouse then drove to the Tavern. She sat at the bar where Ed Taylor, the owner, served her. "New girl in town, right? Welcome to the family you'll get to know here."

"Ed, thanks. I was here last evening and Rachel pointed you out to me. I love the décor of the place. You do love bright colors, don't you?" Silvia sipped her drink.

"Have you moved here, or are you just visiting?" Ed sorted and cleaned glasses then set them to drain until needed for drinks.

"From Boise, but I'm seeking work in Portland then I'll move here. I've waited too long to decide to come out and live among gays and lesbians. I was almost giddy last night just being one in the great crowd. I felt at home; you've probably heard that before." She sipped her drink and looked toward the door, wondering if Rachael would be coming in soon.

"Yes, and have learned many life stories. Thankfully, more are positive stories today but in earlier days, there was a lot of sadness. One young man broke my heart. He desperately needed his parent's approval when he came out, but it never came. He jumped off the nearby overpass in front of an eighteen-wheeler. Thank God, fewer tragedies like that are happening now."

Ed leaned on his arms, looked around for any customers needing to be served; then smiled. "You have a great air of confidence in being who you are, Silvia."

She smiled, "More than at any other time in my life. I've known since my teen years but there never seemed to be the time or place to acknowledge my heart. Now that my kids are gone their own paths, I've found my best path to happiness, I think." Her eyes sparkled.

"I can tell. Good luck to you." Ed smiled, patted his hand on the bar then went to serve other patrons.

Silvia noticed there were only two women in the Tavern; they were playing at the casino games.

All other patrons were men, chatting away with friends. Some were holding hands with the guy at their tables. She saw two guys kiss before they sat at one of the small tables. She grinned. "Ain't love grand." She remembered a time in her life when seeing two guys kiss would have bothered her somewhat. Now it was nice and a smile swept through her heart.

In that instant, she thought about the kiss she enjoyed the evening before. Rachael's lips were soft; so different from the kisses Silvia remembered long ago before her divorce. Rachel walked in.

Silvia waved and smiled, then watched Rachael smile as she walked over. "Hi. I've been here a while; had a great visit with Ed and have been watching the wonderful folks here."

Rachael patted her shoulder. "I was hoping you'd be here. I was delayed when my landlord came by to ask if I wanted the larger apartment at the end of the hall. I was glad for that, so took time to sign the new papers."

"When will you be moving? I'll be glad to help." Silvia watched Ed place a drink in front of Rachael and take her credit card.

"Ed, another for Silvia, too." Rachael smiled and looked into her eyes. "You look gorgeous today. Red's your color." She patted her arm.

"Thank you. I know it's a sunny day but long-sleeves protect me from sunburn. I've had a few melanomas removed from my face." Silvia nodded her thanks to Ed when he set the drink in front of her.

"To answer your question, I'll move next Saturday. That gives them time to refurbish the apartment before I move in."

"Then I might be here to help you; that is, if you'd like. I have to work all week but will come back Friday after work." Silvia laughed. "I don't know how long I'll be driving back and forth every weekend. Maybe a job offer will come soon."

After they finished their drinks, Rachael said, "Let's be tourists. You're new to Portland. There's lots to see here. Let's go to the zoo."

"Sounds great. Let's go."

They walked down to catch the Light Rail Train. "This is a great ride, Silvia, it goes through the mountain then we take the elevator up to the zoo. When we get off the tram, we'll be at the deepest underground light rail station in the world. It maintains a perfect seventy-two degrees. Something special there, before we take the elevator, is a display nearly four hundred yards long. It's a core sample taken from the mountain during construction which is encased in a Plexiglas tube from one end to the other with markings about the age of the earth when each sample developed. It's a geological timeline."

While the train went through the darkness of the tunnel, Rachel started laughing. "Right now, we're below the most famous cemetery in Oregon. The reason I'm laughing, is people got up in arms and tried to sue the City. They were furious that the train would disturb their long-dead relatives. Can you imagine? Such silliness. We're several hundred feet below the graves."

Silvia laughed. "Sure, I can just see grandma in her coffin hearing the rumbling as the train passes through, worrying about earthquakes in the darkness."

At the Zoo Rail Stop, they spent a while studying the core samples and geological information, then took the elevator up and walked down the hill from there to the zoo.

Hours later, they ate dinner in the nice restaurant at the zoo then took the train back to town and the Tavern.

Silvia enjoyed her afternoon with Rachael. She was glad Rachael had not tried to hold hands, nor put her arm around her in the darkened train. Right now, she just wasn't interested in any romance with her new friend or any other woman. Being with new gay friends, and feeling joy in her heart at finally being among gays, was the most special part of her life now. Looking for love and sex was not something she was ready to deal with, not even with her delightful, fun-to-be-with friend, Rachael. In a way, she regretted the kiss, but wasn't ready for more than that.

Someday, she knew, love might find its way to her; now, friendship was special.

That evening, the Drag Queen, Bolivia, led the crowd to laughter and applause in a room half-filled with straight people. It was exciting for Silvia.

Again, Rachael walked her to her car and leaned in for a goodnight kiss. "Bye, Silvia. See you next weekend."

Silvia accepted the kiss. "See you then, Rachael." She stayed at the motel again that evening, made reservations for the same room for Friday, then drove home to Boise.

During the week, Silvia received a telephone call from Portland's United Way personnel director who wanted to schedule an interview for an open position. She scheduled it for Monday with plans to return to Boise for work on Tuesday.

Her week went quickly as Silvia looked forward to her weekend with gay friends and the employment interview. She left Friday at three for the four hundred mile drive to Portland. It might have been a long weekly drive, but it was worth it to her.

At the motel, she showered and changed into her navy blue trousers and a white dressy blouse, then drove to the Tavern where Rachael was sitting with several friends.

They shared a hug and then Rachael introduced her to Diane, Mindy, Robert and Ray.

After her drink was served, Silvia turned to Robert. "Are you and Ray a couple?"

"Yes, we've been together nine years. We met at this very table back then; have been together ever since. What's your story, Silvia?"

"Well, I'm not out anywhere else but here for now, even though I believed most of my life that I was lesbian; my heart told me that. After raising three kids as a divorced woman and single mom, I was alone and focused on my job. Lately, I decided to be who I am, a lesbian. So, I came to Portland to be me."

She spoke with a smile, beaming with pride at her life decision.

"Good for you. You came from where today?" Robert was genuinely interested in her story.

"From Boise. The good news is, I have an interview scheduled for Monday here with United Way; so I may be moving here soon."

Robert patted her arm. "That's wonderful. Good luck."

"Thanks. When I decide to move, I'll tell my kids I'm a lesbian. I don't worry about their response. They and their children are wonderful; they'll stay close. My mom might decide I'll go to hell; but she won't totally reject me. Her way will be silence. Dad's gone already but I sometimes wonder if it would have surprised him. Nobody else really matters." Silvia sipped her drink.

Robert finished his drink, then turned to Ray, "I'm ready to go now; are you?" Ray nodded and they left the table and the bar.

Silvia turned to Rachael. "They're really nice guys. I'm glad I got to meet them."

"I heard you tell Robert how positive you expect your family to be when you come out. It was so hard on him. His father kicked him out and he's never been back. He and Ray have made plans to move to Boston, so they can marry; and they hope someday, to adopt a child or two. They're still young enough to raise children."

"I hope it works out the way they want. I just finished a book about research proving that gays nurture their children better than straights. Of course, the world out there won't believe such research." Silvia smiled. "I do; especially when I meet such nice men as Robert and Ray and Daniel."

"So, Silvia, what's the interview on Monday? I heard you tell Robert you've got one."

"I'll learn more about it when I get there. It's a job in their accounting department. I've got all the skills needed."

The background music changed; then Bolivia performed to a Bette Midler song, "Boogie, Woogie Bugle Boys". The crowd came alive with applause, clapping, laughter and taking tips to Bolivia.

Silvia laughed when Bolivia again opened her bosom to accept the dollar; then kissed her on the lips. She blushed and Rachael teased her.

"No need to blush, Girl; you know he's a nice young man."

"I know but it still embarrasses me." She laughed. "I'm not used to being kissed. Remember, I've been single a lot of years."

"Ah ha, it's the kissing that's got you blushing." Rachael grinned. "What about my goodnight kiss; does that make you drive away blushing?" She giggled.

Silvia blushed again. "Now you've got me blushing again." She focused on her drink, sipping slowly while thinking about being kissed. "You're right, Rachael. I've enjoyed your 'goodnights' to me on the one hand; but wasn't ready, on the other hand."

Rachael leaned away from her. "I didn't realize. I'm sorry." After feeling uncomfortable for a moment, she changed her position again. She leaned her chin on her hand then looked into Silvia's eyes, and waited for her response.

Silvia leaned toward Rachael and spoke quietly.

"Rachael, kissing has always had great meaning for me. I've only kissed my husband back in the days, or my children and grandchildren. Kissing is romantic, is expected when having special feelings for someone; not to a near stranger on our first meeting. I had never had a woman even attempt to kiss me on the lips."

She laughed. "Not being out, I've not allowed my feelings for a girl or woman friend, to lead me to desire a kiss. I know I'm sounding confused; but your first kiss took me by surprise. The second one, I expected. At the same time, I felt friendship for you, but not romance. Heck, I've never allowed myself to even daydream of kissing, or anything more, with a woman. And I never dated anyone after the divorce." Silvia's words sounded apologetically to herself. That wasn't what she wanted to do in her conversation with Rachael, or anybody. "I'm sorry; but I didn't 'come out' for immediate romance and sex, but to just to be among friends and feel as happy as I've been here."

Rachael nodded and looked into her glass. "Silvia, I understand and am glad you've told me your thoughts. I don't know what to say. I'm attracted to you and grateful for our friendship. I guess those of us who have always been out, need to be more aware. I've sensed you're not comfortable showing affection in public. That's why I've not held your hand or put my arm around you when we're sitting here; but a good night kiss? I want you to feel comfortable around me; not wish I'd go away." Rachael raised her face and looked at Silvia. "You're my friend; I don't plan to make you my lover. And, I promise I won't kiss you again without your permission."

Silvia felt tears fill her eyes. "I'm sorry. I didn't mean to hurt you. I'm not some kind of cold fish. Things just have to be slower for me. I'll know when I'm ready for something more."

She lowered her head sheepishly, then looked up at Rachael. "Kiss me goodnight again. You have my permission. Just give me time to know my feelings. Okay?"

Rachael smiled. "We're still friends. Being honest in this conversation means a lot. It's a whole lot better than if you just left me wondering. What I've found interesting about you, Silvia, is that you don't often ask people questions about themselves; questions like when did you come out or have you had a girlfriend before or why aren't you with someone since you've been out a long time. You've not asked me any such questions during all of our hours together."

Rachael waved to the waiter to bring fresh drinks for them.

"That's just not my style. I learned many years ago not to ask personal questions of acquaintances; and it seems to me that when you want to tell me such things, you will. Otherwise, it's none of my business unless we're getting married, or whatever." Silvia spoke with confidence. She knew who she was, and shared what she chose; in turn, she believed others would share what they chose in their own good time. Her mother always taught her that private business was private.

The waiter brought their drinks just as four Drag Queens appeared on stage, dancing and lip-synching in a row as can-can girls. They were dressed comically, more like Raggedy Ann and Andy instead of glamorous ladies.

Two women joined them and introduced themselves as Diane and Mindy. The four of them laughed and applauded the performers. All of them went forward to tip all four Queens.

After the show ended, Rachael walked with Silvia to her car.

"Rachael, where do I meet you in the morning to help you move? I promised I'd help; remember?" Silvia unlocked the car.

"Meet me here at noon. Okay?" Rachel held the door while Silvia got inside, then she leaned in, "Goodnight, dear Silvia."

Silvia turned her face to kiss Rachael. "That was nice. Goodnight."

Rachael stepped back and watched Silvia drive away.

As she had promised, the following day at noon she met Rachael. After finishing their first drink, they went to the apartment building and worked all afternoon moving Rachael to the larger apartment.

When everything was put away and the furniture in place, they sat on the balcony to relax.

"Silvia, it must be expensive for you to stay in a motel every weekend. Why don't you stay here? You can see I have a second furnished bedroom." Rachael wanted to be helpful.

Silvia knew she did not want to be tied to a certain woman, not even her friend, Rachael. If she moved in, there might never be a way to leave; or if she actually met a woman whom she wanted to be with, trouble could brew. "No, but thanks for the offer. I need to stay independent. I don't know what's ahead for me. You're my friend, Rachael, not a lover, and I'd like to keep it that way."

Rachael nodded and chose not to pursue the matter. Besides, she knew she wanted the freedom for a lover if Silvia was going to insist on a limited relationship. "I don't know if you read *Just Out*, Portland's gay newspaper, but a lesbian bar will be opening soon. It's across town. Should be a good place for pleasure and entertainment. Of course, it will build its own clientele. I wonder how it will affect the Tavern."

"Yes, I've been reading *Just Out*. I found a copy at the Tavern last week. I'll definitely check out the new bar."

The United Way interview didn't lead to a job, but Silvia continued to put her application in for various openings. Her luck changed when K-Mart had an opening for a manager. She was able to transfer, thus she did not lose her retirement investment and her salary was higher.

She started her new job the week before a new bar, the Insight for lesbians, scheduled its ribbon-cutting and opening. She decided to go alone rather than arrange to go with Rachael or anyone.

CHAPTER THREE

Jane stood by the oak tree in the back yard and scrolled her finger along the letters, remembering the day Marilyn carved their names. Now she had to learn how to hold and share their memories without breaking down into tears.

The burial was behind her and there were many friends on the patio, enjoying quiet conversation of Marilyn's days in their lives.

Jane turned toward the crowd, smiled, then walked over to be with them. She sat across from Kate and Nedra who simultaneously reached to hold one of her hands. Kate looked into her eyes. "Jane, we know the next days and weeks will be hard for you; but do know, we welcome your call anytime day or night. There will be some evenings you won't want to be alone; when they come, call and we'll be right over. She was the best among us and we have fond memories, not only of her sweet ways but of those times she was the master comic among this wonderful group of friends."

"Thank you, Kate and you too, Nedra. I'm grateful for you and all of our friends. We've all shared some good years together."

Jane dabbed at her eyes with the handkerchief she had been carrying since getting home from the service.

One by one, or by couples, the friends left before the sun went down.

Jane was thankful for all the help she had received that afternoon. She had nothing to do, no dishes to wash or chairs to put away. Everything was in order. She put on a light jacket and went to the car.

It was a pleasant hour, with the sun nearing the horizon and the sky turning dark yellow and orange.

Jane drove to the cemetery and parked near the mound of flowers covering the casket she had seen for the last time; just as she would never again see her precious wife.

She walked over to the grave, knelt and picked up a few of the beautiful flowers. "These, my precious Marilyn, will add a small part of the beauty you always added to our dining table. For a few days, their display will give me sweet thoughts of you and of us as we've been all these years. Honey, I know the sadness will fade, but my memories of you never will. Like Gran shared with me in my dream, that hard chunk of pain inside me is gone because you're not suffering any longer but your beautiful face will never leave my mind. I love you so much. My day will come when I too will leave behind those who love me, just like you and Gran. Until then, I'll hold you close in my heart."

She sat there until the cemetery caretaker signaled it was time to lock the gates.

After her shower, Jane felt refreshed but weary. She quickly fell asleep and rested until the sunshine through the bedroom window awakened her.

She heated a breakfast roll and made hot spiced tea then sat on the patio to eat. From there, she gathered her gardening tools and worked in the flower beds. She talked to the flowers. "You beauties, I hope I can take care of you as well as Marilyn did. She was our flower gardener; I took care of the vegetables." She giggled. "If I treat you like a row of beans and don't give you enough love, you'll have to forgive me."

When the heat of the sun bore down on her, Jane quit working outdoors and went inside to begin to sort Marilyn's clothing. She was a few inches shorter and a couple of sizes bigger, so Jane knew she couldn't wear any of them. By the end of the afternoon, she called the Vietnam Vets to pick up the boxes of things the next day.

Just as she finished a bowl of soup, her evening meal that day, Kate called. "Jane, we just wanted to see how you're doing."

Jane welcomed the call. "Thank you for your concern. I've taken care of Marilyn's flowers and clothing. I've decided to go back to work tomorrow. I think it will be better for me to be busy and among friends."

After the conversation was finished, Jane showered and went to bed.

The following morning, she awoke to the alarm, dressed and went to her job at K-Mart where she was Manager of the hardware department. Being back on a normal schedule, proved to be good for her peace of mind and empty heart.

Four weeks later, to the day after Marilyn's death, the telephone rang. It was Jane's mother, a woman of seventy-eight years.

"Mom, what's wrong?" For years Jane had written to her mother periodically, but never called her, because of the anger her father harbored against her for coming out as a lesbian.

Her mother's tears were audible. "Jane, your father died at six o'clock this morning. They don't know the cause; it was sudden, probably an aneurysm or heart attack."

She began to cry with deep pain.

"Mom, I'll leave right way to be with you. Expect me in three to four hours. Mom, I love you."

Jane's tears fell and she knew they were both for her mother, and for Marilyn. "Mom, I didn't write you about it, but my dear Marilyn died just a month ago, so it's going to be hard for me, but I'll be there for you."

"I'm sorry she's gone. That does make this doubly hard on you, I know. Thank you, Honey, for coming. I need you." Her mother choked on her tears. "See you soon. Good bye."

Jane hung up the phone, sat on the bed and let her tears fall.

She missed Marilyn more than ever; it was as if the phone call was about Marilyn, not her father. His anger and hatred didn't deserve her tears; but Marilyn always would.

After calling her supervisor at home, Jane drove toward Reno, Nevada.

When she arrived, her brother met her at her car. He hugged her, "Sis, I'm glad you're here. I'm so sorry I've not tried to visit you these years. Now's not the time to tell you his threats. Just know, I've missed you and I know Mom has. She's needed you here before, but now more than ever."

"I'm glad I can be here, Todd. And, thank you for seeing that Mom got the letters I sent. Otherwise I couldn't have come today."

Jane's tears in that moment were a mixture of both joy and sadness.

Later, she was to learn details from her brother, about how her father threatened any family member who tried to keep in touch with that 'bitch from Hell.' His ugly words made her glad he was gone.

She stayed a week with her mother before returning to her home and work. When Jane left work Friday at five, she decided to go to the Rainbow for Happy Hour with her friends.

The moment she walked in, Kate saw her and hurried to meet her with a big hug. "You've been missed, Jane. Everyone's asked about you and hoped you were okay."

Other friends lined up to hug and welcome Jane back to their midst. Her heart was warmed as she realized just how wonderful her and Marilyn's friends were. She hugged Nedra, then sat beside her.

Nedra kept her arm around Jane's shoulder. "How's your mom?"

"I talked to her last night; she's recovering. She's never lived alone before; so her life is in a new phase. As a widow, I know what that means. What's different is that my Marilyn was a good and wonderful person; but my father was a mean old goat. He's been so bad to Mom, my brother and the rest of the family who accepted my truth those years ago. He was just plain mean. May he burn in hell for his horrible ways." Her anger was apparent in the gruffness of her voice when she spoke of him.

"Maybe your mom will find the peace, she's never known before. I hope she comes to visit you sometime. I'd like to meet her." Nedra patted Jane's shoulder then picked up her drink for a sip. "It was my Baptist mother who kicked me out. That's when I came to Portland and found the support of new friends here at the Rainbow."

The Rainbow was the oldest gay bar in Portland. It was founded in the sixties by two men, Carl Hampton and Ed Taylor. In those early days, the police were a negative presence, a contrast to recent days when Portland supported their gay community.

By the end of the seventies, Ed had sold his share of the Rainbow to Carl then established the Tavern across town.

Lesbians eventually joined the families in both bars and have become excited that a new bar especially for lesbians, the Insight, would soon have its grand opening.

Three months later, announcements were distributed to announce the grand opening of the Insight. Jane planned to attend the Saturday noon, cutting of the ribbon of the lesbian bar.

She was feeling especially good that morning.

She worked the yard and flower garden during the autumn morning, then showered and dressed for the special occasion. Selecting her white dress slacks and a lacy white blouse, she got dressed, picked up her straw hat and hurried to drive there.

A large crowd had gathered around the entrance at the Insight.

Even though she was sure some of her friends were among those present, Jane had no time to look for them. She stood alone listening to the short speech by Madeline Ramsey, the owner. "I hope the Insight will be home to lesbians from all over the Northwest. It's the first lesbian bar to serve you wonderful ladies. I dedicate it to you and pray you'll bring your friends and meet new friends, and lovers, in the feminine atmosphere created just for you." She cut the gold ribbon and motioned for the patrons to go inside.

Jane followed the crowd and took a seat at one of the tall cocktail tables with a bouquet of roses in the center. A lesbian couple sat at the same table, leaving an open seat between them and Jane. One of them introduced herself and her partner. "Hi. I'm Jodi and this is Marvel. Isn't this a beautiful place?" A lovely, young lady took their orders and soon brought their drinks.

Just as Jane finished the first taste of her drink, someone behind her asked, "Is this seat taken?" The voice was soft, and almost musical like Marilyn's was. Gentle feelings passed through her heart as she remembered the love of her life.

She looked around to answer the sweet voice. Smiling, she nodded 'yes' to the lovely lady near her age with beautiful blue eyes and short reddish brown hair peppered with many strands of silver. "Please do."

Ann Patterson

Jane's heart skipped a beat as she watched her new friend climb onto the stool, and set her small purse in front of her.

"Hi. I'm Jane." She couldn't think of what else to say as she looked into those blue eyes and saw something wonderful.

In her heart, another door had opened to an unexpected future.

Chapter Four

Jane's heart leapt inside her as she watched the lovely woman with the angel-sweet voice take her place on the high stool beside her.

Once she was settled at the tall cocktail table, she turned her face to respond to Jane's smile. "Hi. I'm Silvia." There was gentleness in the eyes, a softness she had never seen before. "Glad to meet you, Jane."

Jane was mesmerized by the soft, almost musical voice of her new friend. She was speechless and never thought to introduce Silvia to Jodi and Marvel.

Silvia turned to the other two women and introduced herself just as the waitress stopped to take her order. She asked for a Greyhound, grapefruit juice and vodka, then turned to Jodi and Marvel. "Isn't this a beautiful place; so very feminine in its décor? Surely today's Opening Day crowd will become the norm here. I know I'll enjoy returning."

Jodi agreed with her. "Like the owner said a while ago, we'll still touch base with the Tavern and the Rainbow at times, just to remind the guys we're still in town to support them. After all, they paved the way for our special bar."

Jane listened to the conversation, still enthralled with Silvia's gentle voice. When the waiter returned with Silvia's drink, Jane said, "I'll get this." The waiter took her money then moved on.

Silvia leaned toward Jane. "Thank you. I'll owe you one." She looked into Jane's eyes and held her in her gaze.

Jane couldn't take her eyes away from Silvia's. "I'm so glad you came to our table. I feel like I've known you somewhere before. I don't know where, but you seem so familiar."

Silvia patted her shoulder. "You have beautiful eyes, Jane. They remind me of the mysterious eyes of the Mona Lisa; they draw me in and make me want to know you more than for just a quick moment."

The soft voice Jane was hearing touched her deeply. She could listen to it for hours.

"Silvia, what's your story? Everyone here in this beautiful place has a personal story. For most of us, our stories are unique."

Silvia glanced at Jodi and Marvel. Seeing that they were absorbed in their own conversation, she felt comfortable focusing on Jane, a lovely woman near her own age.

She wondered how different Jane's story might be from her own.

"I've known since my teenage years in the fifties that my heart turned toward girls, not boys; nevertheless, it was not a time to acknowledge that or I could have not become a teacher, my heart's desire. So, I did the cultural thing, married and had three wonderful children, then divorced. Now my children have gone their own ways, and I've come out. It's a bit late in life for such a decision; but I feel wonderful being among gays and lesbians. I feel truly at home here today, and in past weeks at the Rainbow. Silvia's got a new life and is happier than ever." She laughed. "That's me of course; I don't know why I spoke as if it was a separate person; yet, I have become a new person."

Jane was mesmerized by the soft voice as she listened to Silvia's story. "I'm happy for you. I love the excitement you express at finding your way to this wonderful gay family and community in Portland." She took both of Silvia's hands in hers. "Your joy just bubbles over."

"Thank you. What's your story, dear Jane?"

She looked directly into Jane's eyes, inviting Jane's response.

"I moved to San Francisco for college and stayed there to teach a few years. I always knew my heart was drawn to girls through my school years when the Bay area became the home of a large population of homosexuals, the better word until they used the word, gay. I eventually identified myself with them.

"I met Marilyn and we had many wonderful years together. We moved to Portland six years ago. She died last year and I'm finally past that insufferable grief, and feel alive again. I'll always miss her, but am moving forward. The good Lord closes some doors during our lives; I'm thankful He opens new doors when we're ready."

Jane smiled without moving her eyes from Silvia's; then she picked up her drink and tapped it to Silvia's, "To open doors, whatever's ahead."

Silvia responded to Jane's smile then sipped from her glass. "Yours is a beautiful story. I'm glad you've had such love in your life. The love of my three children sustained me during the years. Now, my life's an open door to whatever lies ahead. Like Auntie Mame in the movie, said, 'Live. Live. Live.' I'm going to live this life with excitement."

Jane laughed. "Wonderful way to be. My new friend, will you join me for dinner?"

"I'd love to. This afternoon has been exciting and wonderful. Where shall we go?"

"There's a nice Greek restaurant nearby."

Silvia and Jane walked to the Greek restaurant, enjoyed getting acquainted, then strolled to the river and walked along the Esplanade, an installed pathway along the river's edge. By the time they returned to the Insight, there were no unshared secrets in their lives.

Entertainment at the Insight included a lesbian comic and the piano bar from which Violet Martinelle, a well-known singer, entertained the crowd until closing time.

At 'last call', Jane and Silvia ordered hot tea and took their time sipping the delicious beverage. Finally, Jane reached to hold Silvia's hand, and moved closer to whisper to her. "Silvia, I know we've just known each other for a few hours. You've enchanted me with you sweet, gentle voice and I can't let you go without knowing I'll see you tomorrow. Actually, I would love to have you come home with me?"

Silvia smiled. "Jane, I've been coming here for months, have had many similar invitations, but accepted none. Your invitation warms my heart; I don't want this evening to end. For the first time, I'm ready to say, yes, I'd love to continue our visit at your home. My little apartment is just too far away from you, my dear woman."

She watched Jane's eyes brighten, and a soft smile cross her face as she nodded her desire to be with the new woman who already had a place inside her heart.

They left together and Silvia followed Jane to her home, parked in the driveway, then waited until Jane closed the garage and opened her car door for her. They went inside the front door of her home.

Walking side by side through Jane's front door, was significant to the two women who had talked earlier about "the good Lord opens new doors after another door has closed."

Jane went to the kitchen and prepared cups of hot spiced tea for herself and Silvia. "I baked sugar cookies today."

She watched Silvia dunk a cookie in her tea. "That's what my Swedish mother always did. You reminded me of her just then. Silvia, thank you for coming with me tonight. Sometimes the house feels so empty; you're a blessing."

"Jane, that's how I feel while sharing your company. You're the one who's a blessing. I came because my heart drew me to you. And, that's so unusual for me. It feels so right to be here with you even though we've not kissed or expressed our attraction in words. It's something deeper than words and kisses. I'm so comfortable and at peace with you and am glad you've not tried to capture me. I just want to be close to you."

"And so we are; close, I mean. I hope you'll sleep beside me tonight. I want to hold you in my arms and dream. It's not my way to just meet and greet then sudden kisses and sex. Whatever I'm trying to say so awkwardly is, Silvia you touched my heart the first moment I heard your voice. I want to be close to you, not scare you in some carnal way but just feel the sweetness you give me." Jane looked at her teacup. "I do have a second bedroom."

"Jane, I do have a car and a choice. I'm drawn to you in a wonderful way. I want to be close with you tonight, and maybe to share a kiss. You know already, I've not made love with a woman; yet I'm open to sharing all you and I choose to share together." Silvia patted Jane's shoulder as she got up to refill her cup.

The cuckoo clock chimed three o'clock. Jane put the empty cups in the sink and set the cookie plate in the cupboard before turning the kitchen light off.

Silvia followed her through the living room and down the hall to the bedroom.

Jane took two silky gowns from the top drawer of the bureau, changed into one and went to the bathroom to brush her teeth and hair.

Silvia watched her then put on the gown. She accepted the packaged toothbrush Jane handed to her. By the time she finished in the bathroom, Jane was already in bed. She went to the other side of the bed and crawled under the sheet, then scooted to meet Jane in the center.

They wrapped their arms around each other and shared a long soft kiss before going to sleep. Two hearts were warmed and each of the women felt love growing in her heart.

Chapter Five

Silvia awakened early when the soft glow of the morning sun slipped through the curtain and warmed her face. When she opened her eyes, she was almost surprised to find she had not been dreaming about having a sweet new friend named Jane.

She smiled, remembering the soft, loving kiss they had shared before relaxing in each other's arms for a deep, restful sleep. Raising her head on her hand, her elbow resting on the pillow, Silvia looked at the beautiful woman next to her. Gently, she lifted a silver curl, twirled in around her finger, and then let it drop.

In that moment, Jane rolled over, eyes open, and looked into Silvia's eyes. "It's true. For a moment, I thought it was all a dream that I had met a sweet, gentle woman who rested next to me all night long." She reached her fingers to play 'piano' with Silvia's fingers. "You're so beautiful."

Silvia leaned to kiss Jane's soft lips, then looked into her eyes. "I'm in the perfect place for me to be this morning. I'm with you, my dear Jane." For a moment, she started to speak those three words she had spoken only to her children in recent years; they fit the moment, the lovely Jane and the warmth of her quickly-beating heart. "Cuddling with you was so perfect. Falling in love with you is amazing; I can't describe what I'm feeling…"

Before Silvia could finish her sentence, Jane reached her hand around her neck and pulled the lovely face closer, so their lips gently touched.

Then, with a smile, she began a kiss that didn't end until Silvia was half-lying on her body, full length with their thighs resting together.

Silvia's thoughts were of love as she felt its grip gently squeezing her heart as her tongue touched Jane's, then played together in increasing passion as her hand felt the warm, soft breast touching her own.

Gradually, Jane rolled their bodies until she was on top of Silvia, her hand exploring the soft curves under the silken gown.

Silvia pulled Jane closer and held her tighter, not sure what would happen next, not wanting to say yes nor wanting to say no. She relaxed in the arms of the woman for whom love was growing in her heart.

Later that afternoon, Silvia and Jane were sitting on the patio, soaking in the warm rays of the sun and enjoying iced tea to keep them cool.

"Jane, your flowers are gorgeous. What a green thumb you have?" Silvia set her glass on the small table and walked down the steps to scan the flower beds.

Jane followed her, smiling as she remembered the many days she watched Marilyn on her knees, plucking weeds and trimming her rose bushes. "Thank you, Silvia, but I can't take the credit for them. Marilyn babied her flowers all season long. I was the admirer then. I'm glad you are now."

She took Silvia's hand in hers and strolled along with her to see the variety of colors and magnificence of the garden surrounding the lawn. "And, now I ask, Silvia, are you a flower gardener too? I hope so."

Silvia flipped a bug away from a yellow rose. "Oh, yes. I love working in flower beds. That's one thing I don't have in my apartment."

"Then, my dear, you've found your place; here with me and working Marilyn's flowers. If you would like, I hope you'll move here, maybe even today."

Silvia turned toward Jane, put her hand on her cheek and smiled. "That would be my joy. Jane, I've never felt so alive and as loved as I have these twenty four hours with you. Nothing would please my heart more, than to be your companion, your wife, your lover." She kissed Jane's waiting lips. "I'm loving you more every moment."

"And, I you, dearest Silvia. Loving you is healing balm to my heart, my life." She wrapped her arms around her new and dear lover. "You're a godsend. I'm so blessed."

Chapter Six

Silvia moved into Jane's home and they began their life as wife and wife in Portland where the gay community had found safety and a haven for their relationships.

Each year the Chief of Police and other Portland leaders participated in the Gay Pride Parade.

Basic Rights Oregon led the way for Equality of Marriage in the state; Portland voters supported the cause, however, rural Oregon voters lead the defeat of Measure Nine.

The year of the negative vote, a leading anti-gay activist, Lon Mabon, created a seriously negative situation. Homemade bombs were tossed into gay bars in the state; however, attentive security guards managed to prevent deaths in those locations.

Basic Rights Oregon continued their mission to educate the voters with hopes for another day when they will approve the right for lesbian couples and gay men, who love each other, to marry and have all benefits of state law.

Many Oregon couples moved across the river to the State of Washington where marital rights had been established.

Silvia and Jane became volunteers with Basic Rights Oregon and spent their weekends together at one of the hundreds of information booths around the state.

Jane was cooking dinner. She called Silvia, "Honey, I need your help for a while. Would you go to Safeway for some colorful sweet peppers for me? I'd like a green, yellow and red one for tonight's meal."

By the time she finished her request, Silvia was at the kitchen door for a kiss; and then she hurried to the store.

Her drive to Safeway was normal. As Silvia walked from the car, she saw a tan pickup, a Ford Ranger with a dirty cover over the bed, park near her car.

Seeing it was nothing special, just a passing thought. Swiftly, she went through the door, nearest the vegetable area, selected three large peppers, self-checked out and returned to the car.

The pickup was still parked and a bearded man sat at the steering wheel.

After parking in the driveway, Silvia went to open the front door. At the same time, she glanced around and saw the same tan pickup pass the house, slowing down for the nearby stop sign.

She shrugged her shoulders and took the peppers to Jane.

She poured herself a cup of coffee and stood watching Jane stuff and cook the peppers. "Something worried me today. I think I was being followed both at the store and as I drove home. It was a tan Ford pickup, kind of dirty and old. I saw it parked in the Safeway parking lot. It stayed there while I went in and out of the store. Then it passed the house just as I opened the front door. I could be wrong, but just seeing it the second time, gave me the chills."

She sat on the kitchen stool and picked up a fresh carrot to munch.

Jane stopped what she was doing. "Did the driver go into the store or what? I'd hate to think we're in some level of danger."

"No, I didn't see him in the store, but as soon as I started driving away from Safeway, he did too. The driver had a short beard; I don't know anyone who looks like him. I hope it was just a co-incidence that he passed the house when he did. Maybe that's all it was."

Silvia set plates and silverware on the table and waited for Jane to put the food there.

They sat down together and began their meal.

Suddenly, a loud blast thundered through the house.

Along with the deafening blast, a strong wind blew through the kitchen, fanning their hair and paper napkins like a March wind and slamming the kitchen door.

Fear filled Jane and Silvia's faces. Something horrible had happened.

They looked at each other. Jane grabbed Silvia's hand and pulled her toward the door, then to the far corner of the back yard where they could see the street.

They heard car doors slam shut and a tan pickup sped away; by the sound of it, they knew it had not stopped at the stop sign at the corner.

"Silvia do you have your cell phone with you?"

Still jolted from her normal serenity, Silvia mumbled, "Yes."

She was shivering from fear and fright at all that was happening, and was unresponsive to Jane's suggestion about the cell phone.

She lay her head on Jane's shoulder.

Jane kept one arm around her terrified wife and took the cell phone from her pocket, then dialed 911. "A bomb or something has hit our house. We were not hurt by the blast but need help right away."

The 911 operator responded, "We've already received a call and emergency vehicles are on their way. Is anyone hurt?"

Jane was relieved they had already been contacted. "No physical injuries, but we're scared beyond reason. We're a lesbian couple and saw a tan pickup three times today. It sped away from here after the blast and didn't even slow down for the stop sign. A bearded man was the driver when we saw it at Safeway. We're volunteers with Basic Oregon and work at their information booth in Washington Square. Maybe someone followed us from there. We've never hidden the fact that we're a lesbian couple. We don't flaunt it either. Like other wise couples, we try to be aware of our surroundings. That's why Silvia noticed the tan pickup."

Jane heard sirens at the corner, then police and fire vehicles stopped out front.

"The police and fire trucks are here now. We're in the back corner of the yard. Thanks for your help. We'll go talk to the police."

She put the phone in her pocked, kissed Silvia and led her toward the front of the house.

The front of their house was in smithereens; blasted apart by some sort of bomb.

They grabbed each other, crying in fear and anger at what had happened.

"Jane, we could have been killed." Silvia's voice cracked as tears filled her throat.

She held tightly to Jane who walked toward the nearest policeman.

"Thanks for getting here so fast. We're scared and angry. We could have died if the bomb had been bigger."

The horror behind her tears, gave the police officer the message Jane's words couldn't speak.

"I'm Sergeant Joe Olson. I'm sorry this has happened. The 911 operator told me you saw a tan pickup with a bearded driver at the wheel. We're already looking for it. I can't imagine the terror you've experienced."

He looked around and saw several of their neighbors running toward them. "How do your neighbors treat you?"

"They're good neighbors. I've lived here nearly eight years and the neighbors have known we're lesbians, but none have ever been unkind. It's a good neighborhood."

Jane wiped her tears with one hand while still holding Silvia close.

Silvia was unable to regain her composure.

She continued to weep and was so weak, she almost fell.

Her grip on Jane's shoulder tightened.

After Sergeant Olson finished gathering information from Jane, he suggested, "Maybe you'd like to go back to your kitchen, and help your partner. Maybe a cup of tea will help her get through the evening. I'll find you there if I need to talk to you again."

She turned to take Silvia to the kitchen.

Police officers kept the neighbors at bay, while other officers began to gather debris in plastic bags, labeling the bags when they were full.

Interviews with the neighbors were conducted, with hopes some of them may have seen not only the tan pickup, but any other person who might have been stalking the women.

Police and other emergency people worked until long after dark, surveying the destruction and gathering scraps of the bomb, the remains of the door and other items for their investigation.

Sergeant Olson told Jane a team of officers would stay at the scene until further notice. She wondered if they thought the bombers might return to finish the deadly attempt on the couple's lives.

Mark Wilson, their next-door neighbor, gathered several men from the neighborhood to shore up the damaged area and cover it with a heavy plastic tarp.

They also gathered the remainder of the scrap wood and glass and loaded it into Mark's truck so he could cart it away the following day.

They were considerate neighbors to the lesbian couple living in their midst. By midnight they had finished their tasks and returned to their homes.

Silvia spent the evening resting to regain her composure in the bedroom, which had not been damaged.

After the neighbors finished their work, she joined Jane in the kitchen for a cup of tea and nibbled on a sandwich.

"Silvia, I'm so sorry, Honey. Nothing like that's ever happened here in our area before; not since I've been here. I'm afraid somebody has followed us from where we worked at the Basic Oregon booth last week. Maybe we need to stop volunteering until the driver of that pickup truck has been arrested; of course, whoever he's working with will know we're still alive. I'm so sorry you've not been safe with me."

She wrapped her arms around her wife. "Why do they even care about who we love? We don't hurt them; and if we get the right to marry, we still won't hurt them or influence their lives in any way. Their hate is so sick."

Silvia was in tears again.

"I know. Their ugly hatred is misplaced. We only want the right to love whom we choose. None of us want to hurt them or their families. Hatred is so horrible and un-American."

She wiped her tears away and drank the hot spiced tea which Jane set in front of her.

Jane went to her kitchen bulletin board at the end of the upper cabinet and un-pinned a paper. "Here's a poem I wrote about it; the hatred, I mean."

She handed it to Silvia.

Silvia began nodding her head as she silently read the poem. Then she read it aloud:

"Hatred"

Coursing with power from evil hearts,

Causing sorrow, pain, torture, even death.

Its ugliness, the worst of humankind

Rushing with destruction, crushing life

From those who love differently.

They boldly say, "God is ours.

He filled us with His love."

Will He turn from them

When they judge with hate,

His creations, now called gay?

Hatred cancels love.

For humankind to love,

For deaths to stop,

For Christianity to survive,

Gay sons and daughters must live;

Hatred must vanish.

Love must win.

When she finished reading, Silvia had tears in her eyes. "A perfect poem. It tells the whole story. It reminds me of the young boy whom Ed, at the Tavern, told me about. His parents kicked him out, and then because of their hatred of their own son, he jumped off the overpass in front of an eighteen-wheeler. Too many have died. God doesn't want such hatred to exist."

Jane put her hand on Silvia's shoulder. "I know. And, that's why those words came to me one day."

She kissed her wife's cheek. "Honey, let's sit on the patio for a while. The police are protecting us and we can relax with the beauty of your flowers. They all are so beautiful; so are you. Let's enjoy the beauty of the moonlight for a while before going to bed."

Jane reached for Silvia's hand and led her out to their chairs on the patio.

After a while, they showered and went to sleep; each in the arms of the wonderful woman who loved from the depth of her heart with hopes the bomber would be arrested.

Chapter Seven

Jane and Silvia returned to their jobs a week after the bombing.

By then, their house was repaired, thanks to a good insurance policy.

Unfortunately, nothing could stop the hate or the fear which had not left their hearts since the bombing.

Jane kept in touch with the police to learn about the search for those responsible for bombing their home. She was told they knew which organization was behind the bombing and similar attacks for which arrests warrants would soon be executed.

After she hung up the phone, Jane turned to Silvia. "Babe, they know who to arrest and will do it soon."

"I wish, Jane, arresting them would stop the hate; but have no confidence in that. People who hate any group in society enough to use bombs and fire and hangings as in the South, don't stop hating. Actually, they get more fired up instead. Why, I wonder, do they choose hate instead of love?" Silvia changed the channel on the television and curled up beside Jane. "I love you and just don't understand hatred."

"I love you, my sweet wife. I wish I could keep you safe from all that, but it's not in my power. We just have to pray and love and hope." Jane kissed Silvia and went to the kitchen to prepare some hot spiced tea for them.

Silvia joined her in the kitchen. "Let's do something special for our vacation this year. Let's go somewhere neither of us has been before. Maybe Amsterdam." She laughed. "I wish we had the money to go to Amsterdam and get married there."

"I wish." Jane poured the tea then sat at the table with Silvia. "Even if we could, Oregon wouldn't, couldn't recognize our marriage. Someday, I believe, all states will have to recognize marriage equality. Maybe, when that happens, Americans will quit finding hateful reasons any two people shouldn't have the right to marry. Remember the Lovings, the African American couple who finally earned the right for interracial marriage. The Supreme Court needs to make a clear decision about marriage that will never prevent any two people who love each other from getting married."

"Think about it. Even if that was the law of the land, those who carry the putrid of hate in their hearts, would find still find someone to hate, fight and kill." Silvia sipped her tea and reached over to hold Jane's hand. "They can never kill the love we share. Our hearts are melded as one, and no opinion or law can affect that."

Jane stood up then kissed her wife. "I do love you, so very much. Other than Amsterdam, where do you want to go for our vacation?"

"I was thinking; we've talked about going to Disneyland. If we did, we could stop on the trip to see my son and grandkids. It's been so long since I've seen them. And, I've not seen the last two grandbabies." Silvia smiled as she thought of her grandchildren. "I'm glad I get to see my daughter in Washington, but I do miss not seeing the other two. I don't know when I'll ever see my daughter in Georgia. Her kids are growing up, only knowing her in-laws there."

"Then it's decided. We'll go south and visit your son too. I've not been to Disneyland for thirty years." Jane finished her tea. "Let's go snuggle under the sheets, dear wife of mine. Maybe we can enjoy some special loving, now that the crisis is behind us and Disneyland's ahead of us."

Silvia followed Jane, turning out the lights as they went to the bedroom. She undressed and began to enjoy the warmth of the shower when Jane joined her. "My Sweetie. It's been a long time since we showered together." She kissed her lover and caressed the curves of her slender body.

****

The first two weeks of September came quickly for Jane and Silvia and they packed their camper for the trip to Disneyland. As she eased the camper onto the street, Jane questioned, "I wonder if we're wise to leave our home empty for two weeks. Of course, the security system will summon the police if something unexpected happens."

"Honey, we can't live like prisoners in our home. We have to trust there's more goodness than hate in this world. Let's just trust God to take care of things while we have a wonderful vacation."

Silvia was anxious for their trip to be peaceful, and knew worrying about their home would interfere with that. "Promise me you won't worry your pretty head about bad things for the rest of the trip."

"I promise."

They drove almost to the California border before stopping for the night. Jane pulled into the parking lot at Seven Feathers in the Canyon, a full-scale casino and luxury hotel. "Let's have some fun at the tables, maybe see the showgirls on stage and even win a few dollars. I'll get us a room first."

When they walked into their room, Silvia was pleased. "This is wonderful. I could spend the whole two weeks here." She opened the curtains and went to the balcony. "A swimming pool too. Thanks for stopping here tonight."

"Do you want a late night swim or a place at the Blackjack table?"

"Let's win tonight and take a swim before leaving in the morning."

Not being in a hurry, since they were on vacation, Jane and Silvia took a late morning swim before heading on to California. When they got near San Francisco, they decided to spend the night in the Castro District where they could take in a Drag Show at Harvey's, the most famous gay bar and club in the nation. Silvia called ahead and reserved a room for them.

After a shower and dressing fancy for going to the Drag Show, the two happy women walked in the crowded showroom.

"Jane, this place is fabulous! So many lights, so many colors and a wonderful crowd."

Silvia followed Jane to a table where there were two empty chairs, and sat down just as the emcee for the Drag Show appeared onstage, glamorously adorned and dancing.

Other Drag Queens joined her, lip-synching the words and dancing to the loud music of Neil Diamond's "Coming to America".

Silvia and Jane introduced themselves to the other ladies at the table and applauded the performers.

Silvia spoke quietly. "This is so wonderful. The first time I told someone I was a lesbian was at a Drag Show. That was the most freeing moment of my life. Now I'm so happy with you."

Jane put her arm around her wife and smiled. "I love you so much."

The following morning, Jane drove south through central California to Bakersfield where Silvia's son lived with his family.

She dialed his number to let him know how close they were.

Following GPS instructions, Jane drove through downtown Bakersfield to the address on Mercury Court. She smiled as she watched Silvia's excitement build as she looked forward to seeing her son again. It had been five years since their last visit. Telephone calls were wonderful, but an in-person visit with hugs to cement the shared love, was the best of all.

When Jane stopped in front of a moderate-sized home with a well-groomed lawn surrounded by flowers, she watched Silvia hurry from the car into the arms of a handsome young man, his wife and three children.

Her heart was warmed at the expression of love between Silvia and her family.

After waiting for Silvia's initial greetings and sharing of love, Jane exited the car and walked up to the group. Silvia reached for her hand, then introduced her to Travis, her son, and his family.

He shook her hand with a welcoming, accepting smile on his face. The same welcome was extended by Joan, his wife, while Silvia was talking excitedly with the small children. She picked up the youngest and turned to Jane.

"This is Tracy. Doesn't he look like his father?"

She kissed her son on the cheek.

The group went inside where Joan served coffee and cookies as the conversations filled the room. Silvia spent half the time sitting on the floor with the small children, getting acquainted with her grandchildren; two of them for the first time.

When Silvia mentioned hers and Jane's intention to leave by dark and travel on toward Los Angeles, her son insisted they spend the night with them and leave in the morning.

Silvia was grateful for his determination because that meant he fully accepted her relationship with Jane.

They stayed overnight, sleeping in the same bed with gratitude for Travis and Joan's acceptance and love.

By noon the following day, Jane pulled into the campground where they opened their camper, purchased wood for an evening campfire then set-up their site as they wished.

Silvia opened bottles of beer for the two of them, handed one to Jane then sat in the chair beside her to enjoy the warmth of the campfire.

"Jane, this has been a wonderful day for me. Not just to see Travis and his family, but to watch them treat you like family. They didn't show a single negative reaction to you or us, even acknowledging our right and desire to sleep together. I am so thankful."

"I know you are. Like your sweet daughter in Seattle, their love for you is the very best. You raised them well. They love and respect you. No parent could want more. I'm happy for you."

"That little Tracy's the spittin' image of his father. I found myself thinking about my children as youngsters and the happy moments we shared."

The campfire turned to red coals and then darkened as Jane and Silvia discussed their day and their lives together. Then they cuddled together in their camper for a welcomed night's sleep.

While Jane cooked breakfast on the camper stove, situated outside the camper, Silvia returned everything inside to its best order. She stepped out just as the sun shone in the camp area. "What a beautiful day for Disneyland. We'll have fun there. I took the kids to Disneyland when they were in their teens. They loved being there and having the freedom to do whatever they wanted. I didn't need to be with all of them all the time, and they loved that freedom." She smiled. "One daughter, my oldest, had a crush on Peter Pan; I saw her talking to him several times. My son went through the new Space Mountain several times. It was a great day for all of us."

"I know teenagers love having freedom. Good moms know when to give it to them. You really were a good mom; that's why they love you so much now." Jane put breakfast on plates and handed one to Silvia. "I hope it's good."

"Of course, it is. You're the cook." Silvia smiled and began to eat.

Jane filled their tea cups before sitting near Silvia and the campfire.

After the dishes were clean and the fire was extinguished, Jane drove them to Disneyland for a day of fun and joy.

Walking together down Main Street at Disneyland, Jane and Silvia enjoyed the daily parade of Disney characters.

They rode every ride except Space Mountain, which Silvia was afraid would be more than she could cope with at her age. "I found it to be too scary with all its sharp turns and downward spirals in the dark when I rode it with my daughter. I don't think it would be any better for me today."

She laughed. "Growing older has made me wiser."

"You're not old, my dear Silvia. You're just wise and wonderful." Jane's confidence in the women she loved was solid.

They stayed for the evening Disneyland activities then drove back to the campground. The following day they went to the nearest beach to swim in the Pacific.

They acted as tourists in the Los Angeles area before driving north, stopping in Bakersfield to see the grandchildren again. The next day they then drove north stopping again at Seven Feathers in the Canyon for their final night on the road.

Arriving home, Jane and Silvia found everything was fine. No damages to their home or yard and a story in The Oregonian that arrests had been made with four people charged in the bombing of their home and for a Hate Crime.

That evening, while sitting on their patio, Jane and Silvia felt safe, that there would be no more danger to them or their home.

After watching the moon disappear behind tall trees, they cuddled together under the sheet and blanket, shared sweet loving, and slept peacefully.

Chapter Eight

A year to the date Silvia and Jane had met, they were planning a special celebration for their anniversary. Problem was, each planned for her celebration event to be a secret up until the last minute. Neither realized what the other had planned, yet each believed things would happen just as she had planned.

June 30, was the wonderful day.

Jane went shopping and selected a wedding ring to present to her sweet wife at their anniversary celebration. She made reservations at the Governor's Hotel for dinner and a room with plans for champagne.

By then, Silvia had purchased a wedding ring for Jane and made reservations at the Oregon Coast Hotel where they could swim in the Pacific and have a special evening for dinner and dancing.

Prior to their anniversary, one evening Jane and Silvia were sitting on their patio enjoying wine colors and chips. Jane smiled and asked, "Silvia, do you think if we hadn't met that day at the Insight, you would be with Rachael now? She's a nice person and was available to you then. Of course, I'm glad you loved me instead."

"Honey, you need never worry. She was my friend, still is, but my heart didn't reach in love to her like it did you." Silvia looked into her sweet wife's eyes. "I love you more every day."

"It was love at first voice, the sound of your voice drew my heart to you. God must have brought you to that empty chair that day. When I looked into your beautiful eyes, I was hooked. I've been thankful every day." Jane leaned to Silvia for a kiss.

Silvia looked at the moon. "My grandmother told me the last time I saw her, 'Silvie, whenever you miss me, look at the moon and remember it's shining on both of us at the same time. We both loved our grandmothers; maybe they brought us together."

"I like the thought of it. Maybe both of them know each other in heaven."

Silvia laughed. "Maybe they are lovers in heaven and wanted us to know the same love."

Jane laughed with her. "Nice thought. Sweetheart, for our anniversary, I wanted to surprise you, but am now thinking I should include you in planning what we'll do. I've called and made reservations on the coast for dinner and overnight stay. Would that work for you?"

"Honey," Silvia said while laughing, "I've made reservations at the Governor's Hotel, Portland's finest, for dinner and overnight. So, what shall we do now? I just want it to be special."

"Me too; shall we do both or flip a coin? Obviously, both of us want it to be special because we're so happy." Jane swatted a mosquito. "Darn mosquitoes. They know how to spoil a nice evening." She stood up to go inside.

Silvia took Jane's hand. "I'd love to go to the coast so I'll cancel the reservations I made. We can leave after work Friday. Will that work for you?" She turned off the outdoor light and locked the patio door.

"It's the perfect time for enjoying sand and sea, as well as dinner and a wonderful room for the weekend." She turned to share a hug and kiss with Silvia.

Friday afternoon came quickly. They were already packed and Jane drove them to perfect weather on the coast. That evening they went to the dining room for dinner and spent the rest of the evening on the dance floor. The leader of the small band asked, "Who's celebrating a birthday or anniversary this evening?"

Silvia and Jane raised their hands at the same time five other couples, heterosexuals, raised theirs. They were pleased when the band leader called on them to tell of their celebration in the same manner, as he called on the heterosexual couples. In addition, he invited them to join the other couples on the dance floor as his band played "The Anniversary Waltz."

Silvia was still smiling when the dance ended. "That was so wonderful; being acknowledged along with others."

Jane waved a 'thank you' to the band leader. "Oh, yes. Anytime one more person treats us like straight couples, it's a joy." She led Silvia to their table, knelt in front of her while removing the diamond ring from her pocket.

"Silvia, you know I love you. Now, I want to put a ring on your finger to remind you that I want to spend the rest of my life with you." She took Silvia's hand in hers and gently placed the ring on her finger. "Forever, my Love." Then she kissed her sweetheart and wife.

Before Jane could get to her feet, Silvia signaled with the palm of her hand for Jane to "stay right there." From her small silver purse, she took the diamond ring, reached for Jane's hand, and then placed the ring on her third finger, left hand. "I love you now and forever. Just as there's no end to this ring, there is no end to my loving you." They kissed again.

The patrons around them applauded Silvia and Jane, smiling and speaking "Congratulations." The band began to play and they joined the others on the dance floor.

At closing time, Silvia and Jane thanked the band leader for his kind attention and including them as he did all that evening.

After sharing sweet, sensual love, the sweethearts went to sleep in each other's arms. Their anniversary celebration had been just perfect.

Chapter Nine

One morning in November, Jane and Silvia were enjoying hot spiced tea while listening to the last birdsongs before the birds returned to Arizona or Mexico for a warm winter.

Only the asters of many colors remained in bloom; all else had taken on the colors of autumn.

Jane reached to place her hand on Silvia's. "I so enjoyed watching old movies on Encore last evening. I hadn't seen "Magnificent Obsession" with Rock Hudson and Jane Wyman for years. For some reason, I remember the afternoon I first saw the movie on the big screen. It was 1954, a hot summer day. By six o'clock that morning, as a fifteen year old, I was in the peach orchard climbing up and down twelve or fourteen foot ladders, picking peaches."

"You did what? I guess you've always been a hard worker. I could never see myself working in the orchards that way." Silvia laughed. "What got you started?"

"I was a farm girl, had picked cotton as a kid. The kind old man who owned the orchard was willing to let me try earning a few dollars. He found out I was strong enough to handle the ladders and do the work. I worked for the same contractor from the time I was twelve until I was sixteen, old enough to work at the cannery.

Anyway, that particular Sunday, I got home by two, showered and went to see the movie. I think the movie itself was the reason I remember the day so well. Last night while watching it on television, I realized it was the message of the movie that cemented it into my mind. The 'magnificent obsession' was a way of life for anyone desiring to live well by doing positive things for other people, just for the sake of doing it; not for personal attention or gain. I think I took the message to heart for I know I've tried to live kindness all my adult life. It's just the right way, reaching out to others in simple ways when they least expect the help they need. Maybe I took that message to the deepest part of me that sunny afternoon."

Jane sipped from her cup. "I don't mean to brag; it's just a revelation to my heart today. An important part of the story was to keep the kind deeds a secret rather than expect applause, something I've tried to do all my life."

"Honey," Silvia squeezed Jane's hand, "you're not bragging. Actually, you're teaching me something. I've seen the movie before and only focused on Rock Hudson and all he means to us as gays. Also, Jane Wyman, who made only one mistake in life, marrying Ronald Reagan, the President who decided to 'let the homosexuals be damned' instead of acknowledging the HIV/AIDS epidemic early enough to prevent some deaths. It took him too long to lead Congress to provide money for research."

"That's the sad truth, Silvia. We owe much to Rock Hudson for allowing the world to know his life's secret and to Elizabeth Taylor for standing by her friend when he was suffering. Women everywhere were disappointed to find their 'heart throb' had never been available since his heart loved men, not women. Even so, Elizabeth helped to wash away much of the shame carried by gays and lesbians. She raised money for AIDS research. If her life had never stood for something before, being his loving friend made her the best ever."

"I'm glad the movie was on last night and I thank you for sharing as you have. Jane, you're the most caring, generous person I've ever met." Silvia laid her head back on her chair and smiled. "I'm so thankful for the love we share."

That evening at bedtime, Jane quizzed Silvia, "Hon, you've got a lump right there." She pushed on the lump she had found in Silvia's left breast. "Does that hurt?" Wrinkles creased her forehead; her heart sank. "You'd better call Dr. Gilcrest first thing in the morning. That needs to be checked out."

"But it's not hurting at all. I'm glad you noticed it, Jane. I promise to call for an appointment." Silvia felt the lump and began to worry.

Neither of them went to sleep quickly that night. Both worried about the lump in Silvia's breast, and like any knowledgeable women, feared breast cancer. The following morning Silvia made an appointment for the next day.

Jane zipped her jeans and tucked in her shirt, then put on a blue denim vest. "I'll be right there with you at the doctor's office. Honey, don't be so worried until we know for sure. Usually, they don't know for sure until a biopsy, and it may not even be required." She wrapped her arms around Silvia and hugged her close. "We'll just pray and believe you've not got the big C."

"I'm trying not to worry, but it's just natural to be concerned. My grandmother and two paternal aunts had breast cancer. Aunt Elva was eighty-one when she had the surgery but she lived to ninety-eight; so I know, it's not always deadly. That encourages me." Silvia buttoned her silky tan blouse and tucked it into her tan slacks. She added a string of pearls then combed her silvery hair. "My hair's turning silver so fast this year. I guess that's what happens when sixty rolls around." She gave a quick laugh, as she picked up her small purse and followed Jane.

After Dr. Gilcrest checked Silvia's breasts, she typed something into her computer then leaned against the wall and looked at Silvia. "It may be benign; however, it's the kind of lump that requires a biopsy. My nurse will schedule you for a biopsy with a surgeon and I'll see you afterwards. Hopefully, as in most cases, it will be benign."

The biopsy was scheduled for three days later; three days that seemed like a year to Jane and Silvia as they waited and worried.

While waiting for the lab report after the biopsy, Silvia was nervous. She sat in her room with Jane nearby, grinding her teeth and fiddling with her finger nails while tears filled her eyes. "I hate waiting."

"Honey, let's hope this waiting will be the hardest part of today." Jane sat beside Silvia, holding her hand.

She was quiet for a few minutes looking at Silvia's worried face. Then, she put her other hand on Silvia's shoulders and bowed her head, touching it to her sweetheart's head. "I want to pray with you right now. The part of me that feels things spiritually, is drawing me into prayer."

Silvia smiled then bowed her head.

"Dear God, I know You're near Silvia and me right now. Only You can meet the need weighing heavily on both of us. I know You love both Silvia and I and that You are the Healer. At this moment, I ask for Your healing hand to touch Silvia's body, her breast, and give her Your miracle of healing she needs today. By whatever plan You believe is best, please heal her from whatever is happening and give her all the physical and mental strength needed today. Thank you for your Love, and for the love You've placed in our hearts for each other. In Jesus Name, Amen."

She hugged Silvia.

"Thank you, Jane, your prayer means a lot."

The surgeon, Dr. McEntire, walked in. "Silvia, the bad news is the lump is malignant. The good news is that surgery can be expected to allow complete removal of the lump. The nurse is scheduling surgery now."

Tears filled Silvia's eyes. She squeezed Jane's hand. "I'm so scared." They left Dr. McEntire's office with fear building up inside both of them.

Two days later Silvia checked into the hospital for the surgery. "Jane, I'm believing your prayer means God will heal this thing, and I'll be all right. I love you so much and want more years at your side."

"Me too." I'll be in your room waiting for the good word and your return from the operating room."

Jane waited; the surgery took an hour longer than anticipated. The moment she saw Dr. McEntire arrive at the door, she jumped up from her chair and hurried to meet him. "It took so long."

"Yes, she'll be out of the Recovery Room soon; the malignancy had spread farther than we expected. Silvia will still need chemo-therapy." He left the room after answering Jane's questions, but he gave no promise of when Silvia would be completely free of the cancer.

After a while, Silvia was returned to her room. Still sleepy, she mumbled to Jane, "Honey, it's not over. I'm so scared." Tears rolled from her eyes as Jane kissed her forehead.

"I know, Hon. Chemo-therapy's awful to deal with, but we'll get through it." She sat beside the bed and laid her head on Silvia's hand.

Memories of having done the same with her beloved Marilyn, settled in her mind. Would she have to go through another death of the woman she loved?

Her tears increased.

They stayed together until Silvia was released and able to return home.

The following weeks were extremely difficult, with the chemo, vomiting and worrying.

A month later, Silvia was back in the hospital for another surgery. Her fear increased and Jane's faith waned. She was there three days, then returned home with a referral to Hospice.

"Jane, you know what Hospice means. It means I'm dying; the cancer is winning. I hate this. I want more years with you."

Jane had no words of comfort. "I know, my darling, I know. In my career I've helped form two Hospices and know they're only for patients with no future. I never expected to have my most loved woman in the world be a patient for any Hospice. I love you so much. It's not fair."

The Hospice nurse taught Jane the details she needed to know about providing morphine for Silvia's pain. Actually, there was no schedule because she was told to respond to Silvia's need for her pain; she was advised about the maximum amount which would be safe during any period of time.

Jane found it hard to accept Silvia's expected death. She had been through such a traumatic time in her life with Marilyn; it didn't seem fair to have to lose a second beloved wife in one life. Every day was difficult.

Silvia's three adult children visited with her when she called for them. With them in the room, she turned to Jane.

Weak and hardly able to speak, Silvia took Jane's hand in hers. "Honey, I'm sorry this happened. The last thing I ever wanted was for you to have to go through this again. If only I could get well instead. I can't, my darling. I'm so sorry. You've been so wonderful to me. And, the way you've cared about my children and family has been beautiful. I want them to know I've loved you with all my heart these few years we've had together. I want them to hear me tell you how important you are to me. I've signed the documents to ensure our home is totally yours. With you in mind, my cremation has been planned. We've arranged for half of those ashes to be sprinkled by you in our flower beds. The other half is for them to put wherever they wish. I've asked them to keep in touch with you and help you whenever you need help of any kind."

She turned to her children. "Please treat my precious Jane with the same love you've given me. She and I have lived as one, as wife and wife in love, and shared so much. Promise me?" She smiled as her son and daughters nodded, and moved closer to her and Jane. "Thank you. I love all of you and will be with you in whatever way is allowed on that Other Side of life. God willing, your lives will be happy even when thoughts of me cross your mind. When that happens, assume I'm whispering in your ears, telling you how much I love you and am grateful to you." Her voice faded and she closed her eyes to rest.

Jane turned to Silvia's children. "Thank you for lending me your sweet mother these few years." She raised her arms to them; and together, the grieving, loving family shared a long hug.

Jane prayed for them to hear, "Thank you, God, for the joy, the privilege and the love we've all had with Your beautiful Silvia, as mom and sweetheart. Please bless her precious children with strength and Your love, in the coming days."

All three children said, "Amen."

A week later, Silvia passed to the spiritual side of life, that Other Side, the unseen and unknown. Her daughter from Seattle attended the memorial service in Portland at the Insight before taking the portion of her mother's ashes allotted for her, her sister and brother.

Jane's life was barren again. After she scattered Silvia's ashes among their flowers, she purchased a burial place in the nearby cemetery for herself, arranged for her own future cremation, then purchased a grave marker on which she listed her own name and date of birth followed by the words "Wife of" then both Marilyn's and Silvia's names. She didn't believe she would have the joy and privilege of being loved romantically as a wife again. Loneliness, she thought, would be her way of living her final years in her home.

Chapter Ten

Jane worked the next two years then retired at sixty-five. Her income reduced significantly, but her house payment was reduced to $675.00, a thousand when taxes and insurance costs, were counted. Social Security was $1,199.00 and the pension from her years of working was $480.00. Medicare-Blue Cross would handle most of her medical costs. Fortunately, she was in good health, as long as medications were available for high cholesterol and high blood pressure. She lived comfortably and traveled very little.

When not taking care of her home and yard with the beautiful beds of flowers, she continued to visit friends at the Rainbow, Tavern or the Insight.

Even there, friends her age were dying off, and younger gays weren't interested in their elders; that is, except for the New Year's Eve when she dressed up to celebrate where her favorite Drag Queen still performed.

Jane had her hair trimmed and sported a chic new hairstyle. She smiled at herself in the mirror. "You're looking fantastic tonight, girl," she told her reflection in the mirror. Wearing her bright Christmas-red sports jacket, black slacks, white long-sleeved shirt and the necktie-styled rhinestones, she looked vibrant, and even young.

To add to the festive appearance, she added the jeweled silver cover over her shoulders. It gave a dress-western look to her jacket. "You look spiffy." She smiled, picked up her wallet and keys then went to the Rainbow to dance with the crowd.

It was a clear winter night and traffic was heavy, but manageable. Jane parked in a fee-to-park lot, and found it cost fifteen dollars instead of the normal six dollars. Since it was just a block from the Rainbow, she paid the fee and left her car there.

Because Portland, in fact all of Oregon, had a no smoking policy, there was a crowd outside the Rainbow, more than ten feet from the entrance, enjoying an interlude for cigarettes by 'having a smoke'.

Jane stopped to talk with Rachael, who had just lit her cigarette. "Hey, Rachael. You're looking smart tonight."

"How are you, Jane?"

"Healthy and out to enjoy the celebrations tonight; I haven't been out for an evening since Silvia's death; so tonight, I thought I'd see if these old feet can still move." Jane laughed.

"She was special. I'm glad you two had some good years together." Rachael was still Jane's friend although neither had romantic thoughts about the other.

Jane found an empty seat facing the dance floor. She sat there drinking her Cherry Coke until the dance music began. During that time, a few acquaintances stopped to chat.

The Musak played loud and continually with its constant beat. Most of the dancers were young gay guys; some had a partner while others just danced with whoever was facing them at any moment. Same with the lesbians; most did not have a particular dancing partner.

Jane joined the dancing. She laughed with those who danced around her, smiled at those who smiled, and had fun just being there with good energy and having fun. Several times, the young gay guys asked her to smile for their camera, or photographed her with their loving partner, husband. Those were the ones who seemed to appreciate her the most, because they said things like, "I wish my grandmother would meet my husband and dance with us" or "You remind me of my grandmother." Jane appreciated their attention and their hugs. She found it interesting that most lesbians on the dance floor didn't respond the same way; although one lesbian paid her more attention than she did the girl she was with.

The Musak stopped and the crowd began to leave the Rainbow.

Jane sat at an empty table to have a final drink to celebrate her wonderful evening. While she sat there, a woman near her age, went to her and asked, "May I sit with you to finish my drink?"

The question was familiar. It brought back a sweet memory to Jane's heart. She smiled, "Please do."

"I'm Emily. I haven't danced tonight, but I've been sitting up there on the second deck, watching you have lots of fun. I didn't have the nerve to join the dancing crowd."

Her hair wasn't as white as Jane's, but it was filled with silver streaks along with her reddish strands. She was wearing a lovely blue knit suit and a strand of pearls above the neckline of the suit.

Jane saw Emily's clear skin from the pearls down to a bit of cleavage; a sensual thought passed through her mind. She smiled. "I'm Jane. It was fun dancing with the young people tonight. I hadn't expected to be so appreciated from so many young men; what was nicest, was the joy my presence seemed to give them. They said I reminded them of their grandmother and wished she would dance with them as I did. Those thoughts are worth a million."

"I could tell they loved having you there. So many of them took photos with you. I especially liked the couple who took pictures of each other with you. They loved you; I could tell." Emily's played her hand against her pearls. "Jane, I wanted to meet you; not just now, but maybe tomorrow we could go to the zoo, or somewhere, talk and get acquainted." She looked down at her drink while waiting for Jane's response.

"That sounds great. Shall we meet here or shall I pick you up. I live in the St. Johns area." Jane smiled and patted Emily's hand.

"It would be on the way to Washington Park from there, so I'd be happy for you to stop by for me. I'll write my address down." Emily took a pen from her mid-sized black purse and wrote the information for Jane. "It's easy to find at the corner of Fifth and Davis. I'll wait out front of the apartment at twelve. Let's plan on having lunch at the zoo."

Before the doors closed, Jane and Emily left the Rainbow.

As she got into her car, Jane was still smiling.

Maybe being alone the rest of her life was not inevitable; maybe there would be happier days again. Joy began to fill her heart while her thoughts of Emily joined those of Silvia and Marilyn.

Jane slept well, the rest of the night and awoke to a happier new year. She would have added a live bouquet of flowers to the dining room table if it were spring instead of winter. She found herself singing happy songs as she straightened the house.

Emily was waiting on the corner when Jane arrived. "Good to see you, Jane. It's a lovely winter morning to go to Washington Park and the zoo. The dining room there serves wonderfully during the winter season; and there are many zoo animals and fowl to see in their winter environment." She was excited being with a lesbian her age, as was Jane.

Both women knew how difficult or impossible it was, to meet a single lesbian in their age group. Both felt truly fortunate.

Jane parked in the lot and the two of them bought tickets for the train. They had so much to share about their lives, so neither was bored as the train took them through the tunnel to the zoo stop. Lunch was a good experience as they became acquainted.

Jane appreciated Emily's high energy and apparent good health. She found herself saying a silent prayer, "God, if You mean for us to have a long relationship, please keep Emily as healthy as she seems today. I just can't lose another love of my heart. Amen."

After their hours at the zoo and having lunch, Jane and Emily returned by train to the car. Jane started the motor, "Emily, let's go to the Insight. Have you been there?"

"A couple of times. I just don't drive across town very often. Let's go." Emily's smile proved to Jane just how much Emily was enjoying their outing.

Jane looked forward to sharing time with Emily in a place where she could hold her hand; even kiss her slender fingers, while having a drink. She drove to the Insight.

It was a quiet late afternoon at the Insight. Jane hadn't been there for a long time. She didn't know anyone at the tables nor behind the bar. She took Emily by the hand, and led her to two stools at the end of the bar. Being at the bar instead of tables, made being together much cozier, and holding hands a natural thing to do.

Jane wanted to touch Emily, not just be with her. She believed Emily had the same desire.

Their drinks were served and they sat close together, shoulders touching, as they began to sip their drinks. Heads close, they continued to share about their lives and the day's experience.

Jane put her arm around Emily. "If you're feeling what I am today, this is the beginning of something more beautiful than just a day at the zoo. Emily, I'm happier than any lesbian in Portland. I didn't expect to meet someone special again; but know I have."

Emily looked into her eyes and smiled. "Me to, Jane. My heart's jumping inside me. Being with you is more than wonderful. I don't want this day to end."

Jane leaned in and kissed Emily, slowly. She didn't want the sweet kiss to end. Then, she looked into Emily's eyes. "How long must we wait to take things to the next level? I so want more of you, with you?"

Emily smiled. "Only as long as it takes to be alone, together."

"Let's go to my home. I want to show you where you can spend the rest of your life, if you so decide." Jane patted Emily's cheek and smiled.

Emily giggled. "My glass is empty. Let's go."

Two happy new lovers walked out of the Insight.

Jane drove to her home, parked in the driveway then led Emily inside. "Meet your new home; I do hope you like it."

"I already love it because you come with the house."

Jane kissed Emily then led her down the hall. "My dear sweet woman, please join me in the shower. I want to kiss you under the warm water, and spend hours rolling in the bed with you. I'm so happy; I can hardly wait to feel our bodies together because our hearts are already woven together. I feel that wonderful excitement of falling in love again; and it's absolutely wonderful."

"For me too, dear, dear Jane."

Moments later, they stepped into the shower and began to share a kiss as the warmth of the water flowed over them. Jane smiled as Emily's loving hands embraced her, drawing their bodies together as their hearts grew with shared, wonderful love.

Another door of love had opened to Jane.

Part Two

Stories of Women Loving Women

On the Beach

Janice left her car on the lot and walked down to the beach where she sat on a log to enjoy the scenes around her. The white crested waves moved slowly toward her as they faded onto the shore, disturbing the smooth sand. At the horizon, a ship was passing and puffing smoke that blended with the white clouds above.

Janice scanned the beach where she saw mothers wearing bikini's playing in the sand with their children, duos of lovely bodies gaining a suntan side by side on blankets and there was one gorgeous beauty sitting alone.

In that moment, the beauty looked her way wearing a sweet smile under the brim of her straw hat. She was several yards away from Janice but her blue eyes shone, and her blond hair was blowing in the same wind that lifted the brim of her hat. Janice swooned and her heart skipped a beat. Never, she thought, had she seen such a perfect woman in all her life. She placed her hand on her heart and took a deep breath as she thought how sweet it would feel if she was under the sheet with the tanned, slender body blending with hers. She looked at the horizon again then back at the amazing beauty.

At that moment, her beautiful 'heartthrob' waved her hand.

Janice nodded, walked to her and sat on the sand beside her. "Hi. I'm Janice." Her voice was almost a whisper as she looked into the face, now very close to hers. Janice smiled and felt trembling sensations flowing within her. It was as if love's flower had just bloomed and filled her heart.

"Hi. I'm Lindy." She smiled, putting her hands on the sand beside her and looking into Janice's honey brown eyes. "I was watching you. Then, when you looked my way a second time, I knew we had made a connection."

Janice leaned her forehead toward Lindy's and whispered. "If you mean the 'connection,' I think, for me, it will last forever." She winked. "I love your hat. It speaks of sweet femininity and beauty which are the qualities I first saw in you. Do you come here often?"

Lindy lifted her face toward Janice. "My first time to visit Hawaii and first hour on this perfect beach. Before I saw you looking my way, I was admiring all the lovely bodies in bikinis here today. You know what I mean." Her long blond hair fell toward the sand, framing her face. She smiled and winked.

"Same for me. I decided to stay at the Royal Hawaiian. It's so much smaller, than my grandmother said it was when she came here in 1959. She was a college student then, and the Royal Hawaiian was the grandest hotel in the Islands. It still has some of the elegance she described."

Janice looked at the bright pink building behind her. "And it's still as pink. So much different than the really big modern buildings without personality."

Lindy smiled as she laid one side of her head on her knee and looked at Janice's face. "You're so pretty, Janice. I could crawl right into your eyes; they're so inviting. I hadn't planned on meeting a special somebody so soon. I just arrived yesterday evening from Seattle."

She moved to look toward the ocean and propped her chin on her knee. "I can't believe what I'm feeling right now."

A perfect smile crossed Janice's face as she put her hand on Lindy's back, feeling her soft tan. "Me either. I just know, Lindy." Her fingers played softly on the smooth skin. "We can sit here wondering, or we could go to a more private place to be together."

Lindy looked around. Then she started to stand up, "My room or yours?"

"Either. I've got a great view of the ocean." Janice got to her feet.

The two lovely women, new friends and sharing a special attraction, walked through the lobby to the elevator. Janice punched the button to the fourth floor where her room overlooked the ocean. She unlocked her door and held it for Lindy to go in ahead of her. "Would you like a glass of wine or a coke?" I've got both in the room refrigerator."

"Wine would be great. Not that I need to relax. Just being with you has me so relaxed, I feel like I'll fall down." Lindy went to the door to the balcony. "Nice view. You must have booked your room before I did mine. I can see Diamond Head from mine." She turned and watched Janice pour glasses of wine.

After handing Lindy one of the glasses, Janice unlocked the balcony door and opened it. Instead of stepping out to the balcony, she turned to Lindy, looked into her eyes and smiled. "I just have to kiss you right now, if..."

Before she could finish her sentence, Lindy's lips covered hers. Slowly and gently, she kissed Janice

"Hmmm, so nice." Lindy looked into Janice's eyes and kissed her again, longer until their tongues touched.

In that instant, both women felt a wave of excitement move through them.

Simultaneously, both Lindy and Janice set their glasses on the table and wrapped their new love in their arms.

The kissing continued as bikini straps loosened and the tops dropped to the floor. Soft lovely breasts were gently touched, and nipples grew toward the others so near. Hands softly moved up and down the backs and shoulders of new lovers as Lindy and Janice became one in love and sensuality. Hands pushed the bikinis toward the floor and held the cheeks they had covered, feeling the softness of un-tanned skin.

Moments later the new lovers were on the bed sharing kisses to breasts, belly, thighs and lower; at the same time Lindy put her hand to Janice's wetness and her lips sought the slit as Janice was finding, feeling and kissing Lindy's. Slowly, each of them felt wonderful churning through her body, lips to lips, lips to clit, until suddenly at the same moment, both lovers felt passion explode through their bodies.

They began to relax, as each lover softly touched and brushed her hands and lips to secret-no-more places.

For Joy

Joy Brennan's smile gradually widened as she listened to Senator Clair Kendall explain why she could no longer be against marriage equality. Joy had gone to school with Clair and knew her to be a fair and just teenager; now she had reason to be proud.

Senator Kendall quoted the Bible verse, "And now faith, hope, love, these three; but the greatest of these is love." She went on to reference her gay and lesbian friends and acquaintances at work, even among her staff personnel, who over the years have remained true to their partner in long term, committed love.

Joy had been one of those staff members for the positive, energetic Senator. When she had introduced her sweetheart of nine years to the Senator, she appreciated the kindness received. Now, the Senator said, "I find myself unable to look them in the eye without honestly confronting this uncomfortable inequality."

Joy's cheers could be heard above the crowd. She thought to herself, "Now, when I talk to the Senator, I won't feel judged or condemned because my heart loves a kind, sweet, wonderful woman."

She moved away from the cheering crowd, and dialed her sweetheart, Alice. "Honey, wonderful news. Senator Kendall is for gay marriage. Finally, after so many years since I introduced you to her, her heart blesses ours. I'm so happy, I'm about to burst."

Joy had to move the cell phone away from her ear as she listened to Alice's cheers.

Alice settled down long enough to say, "I can hardly wait for you to get home so we can celebrate together. It's wonderful news. Every time one more person says 'yes' to us, the day of freedom to marry gets closer. I'm excited!"

"I've gotta go right now, but we'll celebrate tonight. I love you."

"And I'll love you forever," said Alice before Joy clicked the phone off and hurried toward her office.

****

Joy had met Alice quite by accident nine years earlier.

It was when Joy pulled out of a parking lot on Main Street in St. Louis, Missouri. The car she hadn't seen, crashed into her fender. She pulled back into the parking space and got out to inspect the damage and deal with the other driver whom she suspected would be irate.

The other driver had stopped, gotten out of her car and was checking for damage to her car. Fortunately, her bumper took the brunt of the hit and wasn't damaged.

Joy watched the slender, brunette walk toward her as her 'gaydar' went into high gear. Her heart smiled; she could feel the warmth flow through her.

Joy's first response was to take a close look at the damage to her fender. She knew she was 'in the wrong' and had no defense. If only she had looked back more carefully before pulling out. She rose up to look into the indigo blue eyes before her. "Hi. I'm Joy Brennan. I'm sorry I've interrupted your day."

Wearing jeans and a shirt like Joy, Alice looked at both cars. "No damage to mine; it's a metal bumper, got a little paint from your fender, but no damage. I'm Alice Bartley. Parking lot bumping seems to be a game here. This is the third one I've seen this week. When the first one happened, I was nearby, and watched the two male drivers have a fist fight. Both blamed the other." She laughed.

Joy laughed with her. "I'm not in the mood for a fight. I prefer to make friends."

She took her wallet from her hip pocket, shuffled through some cards, then handed she handed Alice a card. "Here's my insurance company. If you need to have that paint cleaned off professionally, call him. I'm so sorry."

"I don't see a problem." Alice looked at the card, then said, "Joy, nice name. I think I've seen you somewhere before. Would it have been at the Rainbow?" She named the nearest gay bar in town.

Joy nodded. "Could be. I go there often but don't remember seeing you there."

"Usually I go to The Rose. It's closer to where I work. But occasionally, I stop at the Rainbow instead." Alice laughed. "Actually, the reason I mentioned the Rainbow was to find out if you might be a lesbian since I am."

"I've done that too. Yes, I've been out since college. Where's your partner?"

Joy leaned against her car putting one foot on the tire behind her.

Joy gave a little giggle. "Oh, now you want to know if I'm single. Fact is, I am. I was going with someone, but she moved to San Francisco last month. I miss her but don't plan on moving there."

Joy looked around. "We need to move our cars so others can use this lane. It's such a crowded parking lot. I'll pull back into the parking space."

Alice said, "Why don't we go into the coffee shop over there?" She pointed to the small cafe. I'd like to talk to you a bit longer. What'd you think?

"Sure. I'd like that." While moving her car, Joy found herself wondering if she had just met the 'special someone' she'd hoped for. She had come out to herself as a lesbian two years earlier, but waited more than six months before telling another person, her sister. Now all her friends knew she was gay.

When Alice came toward her, Joy couldn't keep from smiling.

The two strangers, now new friends, went into the cafe and ordered coffee.

Joy wrote some information on a cafe napkin. "Here's my information in case you need to tell your insurance agent."

Alice looked at the napkin and smiled. "I have no reason to do that but I'm glad to have your phone number. Don't worry about my car."

"Thanks, Alice. Your kindness is appreciated. When did you come out?" Joy smiled and sipped her coffee.

She looked around the cafe. It's was decorated like the fifties with black and white checkered tiles on the floor, collectibles on shelves, ancient Coca Cola ads framed and nicely displayed.

The man behind the counter might have been sixty, but he looked like an aging "Fonz" from "Happy Days."

"I came out to myself two years ago." Joy smiled and ordered a coke. "You want a coke?"

Alice nodded and they waited for the clerk to fill their glasses. After they had their cokes and sat down, she grinned. "Second question. Are you busy Friday night? If not, I'm asking for a date."

Joy laughed. "I was just thinking about this fifties' place. Back then, nobody even said the word 'lesbian' and never heard of 'gay' instead of 'homo'. Now two lesbians sit here talking like 'normal' people who've met accidentally but not on purpose. Friday night, when and where? Do you want me to pick you up?"

"No, I'll be at your place at seven. I have your address and your car may still be in the shop." Alice laughed. "I didn't want you to think I was rushing things; but since we're 'family' and go to the same bars, I hoped you'd say yes."

"If you hadn't asked, I was planning to." She sipped her coke.

They talked about their cars, and other things until their glasses were empty.

Alice looked at her watch. "I'm late for an appointment, so had better go." She opened her purse.

Joy put her hand on Alice's. "I'm paying. I'm so thankful you weren't ticked off at me; and I'm gloriously happy we've got a date. See you Friday."

Joy watched her Friday night date walk toward her car. She felt a sweet tremble pass through her insides and knew she had met somebody very special.

Friday at seven, Joy was ready to walk out the door when Alice arrived. She hurried to the car when Alice pulled into the driveway. "Hi. You look great. I love your earrings, little cuckoo clocks. No wonder you're right on time." She laughed. "I've never seen earrings as cute as those." She admired Alice's long wavy hair framing her beautiful face and winning smile. Warm sensations swept through her heart. Love had begun.

Alice laughed. "Glad you noticed. The magic is that they keep good time; the alarms go off inside my brain. Your earrings match your eyes, indigo blue. So lovely."

Joy's earrings had dangling chains, each with several blue stones.

Her medium-length hair was parted on the right then fell smoothly around her face, almost covering her left eye. Her eye make-up was perfectly applied. She wore a navy skirt with a red, high collared silk blouse with lipstick that matched.

"Thanks. I get that sweet comment every time I wear them. Sometimes we're lucky to find the perfect earrings. I did with these." Joy smiled as she watched her beautiful date stop for a pedestrian. "Where're we going tonight? Surprise me." She laughed.

"First stop, my dear, is dinner on the hill. The new Carmen's Restaurant serves wonderful food. From there, we'll decide. I'd like to dance the night away with you." She smiled and winked at Joy.

"Perfect. Sounds romantic as well as fun." Joy moved closer to Alice. "You've got some kind of magnet on me. I've had you on my mind all week."

During their meal, Alice and Joy learned about their lives, work and dreams. When they finished, Alice drove to The Rose, the lesbian bar with a dance floor and live music.

From that date forward, neither Alice nor Joy dated any other woman. Their hearts were sealed with the love that had begun that week.

****

Joy rushed home that evening, burst into the house and grabbed her sweetheart in a long hug and kiss. "Another great day for lesbians and gays. Senator Kendall and Senator Warman both spoke for us today. That's two more Democrats with open minds and hearts."

She laughed and jumped up and down. "I'm so happy!"

Alice laughed with Joy. "More will come. It's too bad the Republican Senators are so silent. Only Senator Portman has been willing to take a stand. God bless him. I hope things will change enough by the time of his next election to keep him in the Senate."

"I'm optimistic." Joy kissed Alice again. "I've got you forever so I'm staying optimistic about everything." She hung her jacket in the closet and turned back to Alice. "How're we going to celebrate tonight?"

"I think we should go dancing; just like on our first date." Alice smiled. "Our love began then, and one day we'll be able to get married. We'll drink to that tonight."

Joy wrapped her hands around the 'wife of her heart' and looked straight into her eyes. "I love you so much, my sweet Alice." She kissed her long and softly.

Ann Patterson

98

Torrent of Tears

One by one, Karen's weeping tears dropped to the ground. Her sight blurred. "Grace, I miss you so much. Our years together could be written as the wonderful love story it was." She pulled another dandelion plant and threw it in the box with all the others that had turned the garden into a weed patch, so different than the manicured garden planted by Grace, her life partner for seventeen years.

Karen had put off the gardening almost a month since watching the beautiful rose-colored coffin being buried in Paoli's cemetery on the hill which she could see at the horizon. Oklahoma's red clay and gravel was just as red in the garden as the mound beside the coffin that day, a reminder of the myth that its redness symbolized the tears and suffering of America's Native people when they walked from their home in Florida to Oklahoma a century earlier. The government was cruel to have done that to them, just as the cancer was cruel to her beloved Grace.

Grace and Karen had worked the farm as a team. They looked alike in so many ways people often thought they were sisters. Their tall stature gave them a special elegance, highlighted by long blond, wavy hair which they wore in ponytails when working on the farm. Each had fine, almost perfect facial features, especially when they donned make-up to accent their lovely blue eyes and big smiles. At the gay bar in Oklahoma City, they had been admired and appreciated as they led in the fun at monthly dance competitions.

The sadness of losing Grace after the horribly, painful illness with brain cancer of so many weeks, remained buried deep inside Karen where she had hidden it while Grace suffered.

Grabbing the green leaves of a plant that had already produced flowers ready to turn to seed, Karen pulled the large turnip from the ground, then she laughed. "I'm silly to even bother harvesting these. This one's too overgrown to have any flavor left, and it's so darn spongy. Grace, you'd be teasing at me this very minute. You'd remind me I'm a better gardener in the produce department at Safeway." She laughed again.

Not understanding why she was laughing, Karen questioned her sanity. In the next breath, the laughter turned to more weeping, then to crying aloud and heaving until her stomach hurt. "Oh, God, I miss her so much."

****

Seventeen years earlier, Karen had attended the memorial service of her grandfather in Paoli, a small town an hour's drive south of Oklahoma City.

Accompanied by a friend, her cousin Andrea had arrived to be with the family the day of the funeral.

After the burial, Andrea had invited Karen to ride in her car where she introduced Karen to her friend, Grace. "Karen, I think you two have a lot in common, so I wanted you to meet. You're both very special women."

"I'm glad to meet you, Grace. I don't know what my cousin has told you about me. We've always been great friends and always shared our

secrets." Karen shook Grace's hands and blushed. She wondered if Andrea had told Grace about their long ago conversation, the one about her confusion when she questioned whether she was a lesbian.

She looked at Andrea, seeking an answer; then smiled when Andrea winked at her. Her response was to 'mouth' noiselessly at Andrea, "You're so clever."

She turned to Grace. "Any friend of this wonderful cousin is a friend of mine. Andrea and I had a world of fun together as kids on our grandfather's farm. Did she tell you about the day..."

Thus began a true romance.

By the end of that day, Grace and Karen had formed a special bond and made plans to meet at Grace's home near Oklahoma City, a week later.

The more the two of them were together, the greater the bond of love in their hearts.

For the next seventeen years, they lived on Grace's farm where they told neighbors and others that they were cousins.

In truth, they shared a beautiful, deep and wonderful lesbian romance as a couple.

****

Now Grace's garden had become Karen's place for sorrow's tears to flow. Her body ached as her tears fell to the soil worked by Grace's hands for so many years.

The release through the torrent of tears was finally demanded for Karen's ultimate survival; hidden tears poured through her, releasing her soul and body to live another day.

There was something about pulling up that huge turnip that allowed her sadness to escape in the torrent of tears.

The barrel of burdens caused by the illness and death were left in the garden that day. It was as though Grace was now beside her, caressing her soul.

Almost fifty and thankful Grace had put the ownership of the farm in both their names, Karen decided she needed a simpler life. She sold the farm to move to California where Andrea and her second husband were spending their retirement years.

The day she arrived, Andrea met her at the Sacramento airport. "I love you, Cousin. You'll love California. There's so much more freedom for people here than Oklahoma would ever allow." They hugged and hurried to her car.

"Andrea, I've always wished we could live closer together; now we will. You gave me the best gift anyone could ever receive. You brought Grace into my life. I still miss her, but now I'm ready to live and find happiness like she'd have wanted."

Andrea smiled. "And, when you're ready, I may have another friend to introduce you to."

"Why does that not surprise me?" Karen laughed. "I don't want to rush into a relationship though. If I couple with another woman, she'll have a lot to live up to; Grace and I were so perfect for each other."

For a moment a veil of sadness filled her eyes and her brow wrinkled. "So perfect."

Andrea remained silent, knowing Karen's thoughts had turned inward to her memories of Grace. She knew to intrude on that moment would have been unkind.

"Andrea, you have a wonderful place here." Karen carried her suitcase to the bedroom Andrea had prepared. It was hers for as long as she wanted to stay until she decided where she wanted to live.

The moving van wasn't scheduled to arrive for another two weeks.

Andrea went to the kitchen to check on the roast which she had put in the oven before going to the airport. It was ready to go on the table with baked potatoes and other items.

As she took it from the oven, her husband walked in with a bouquet of roses. They shared a kiss and she put the roses in a vase then in the center of the table.

Karen walked in. "Roses for your wife. How wonderful." She smiled at him then turned to Andrea. "Looks like you found the perfect mate the second time around. I hope I can be as fortunate."

"I believe you will." Andrea smiled then introduced her husband to Karen. "If you two are ready, the feast is on the table."

Karen's first two weeks in Sacramento were busy ones. She searched for her new home and decided to live in Davis, a town enhanced by the agricultural emphasis at the University of Davis. The home she purchased was just outside the town on four acres which would serve as a garden and a horse pasture. She and Grace had owned horses, rode them often and paraded with other horse owners in various towns. Even though she had sold their horses in Oklahoma, she knew she would buy two for her life in California.

The moving van arrived and Andrea helped Karen get everything in place. The friendship between the two cousins was close and lasting. Having Andrea with her during that period of her life, helped Karen continue to move forward, rather than living in the past and its loss.

Karen attended the annual Rodeo in nearby Woodland and joined the riding group soon after establishing her home in Davis. She had always enjoyed being with horse owners. She had named her place the Bar-K.

After a while she found a lesbian bar, The Blue Lily in Sacramento. She went there occasionally, especially those days she was missing the company of lesbian friends. Accepted quickly as a friend among many she found joy in their company. She appreciated that none of the new friends there 'hit on' her; instead they kept their interest in her beauty and personality, as true shared friendship. When she was ready, and the right lesbian friend touched her heart, she would know, and they would too.

In early Spring Karen's riding club scheduled a ride in the Davis Easter Parade. Karen took "Playmate" with her for the parade ride. Playmate was a black mare with a long mane and tail. While she saddled Playmate for the parade ride, a tall woman with long black hair and blue eyes walked over to meet Karen.

"Hi. What a beautiful mare. She matches me more than Honey, my pinto does." She laughed then reached her hand to Karen. "I'm Joy Kimball."

Karen shook her hand. "Karen Morgan. This is Playmate and you're right; she does match you. I bought her at a sale in San Mateo last month." She turned to continue brushing Playmate's mane.

Joy held the bridle reins of her pinto while she rubbed Playmate's velvety nose. "Honey and I've been in Arizona for the winter parades, so I haven't met you at earlier local events. How long have you been in the area?"

"Since last fall," answered Karen. "I sold my farm and moved here after my partner died. We were very active in the riding world in Oklahoma." She moved to brush Playmate's long wavy tail.

"I'm sorry about your loss. I know it had to be hard on you. Been there; know the pain. My sweetheart died two years ago of breast cancer. I still miss her."

Joy had purposefully mentioned 'her' so that Karen would know she was a lesbian.

"It's not the best thing to have in common, Joy, but my Grace had brain cancer." Karen turned toward Joy. "We never get over losing them to such a terrible disease. My cousin had remarried and moved to California. I sold out in Oklahoma, and now love being here." She finished brushing Playmate, took her rein and led her into the shed.

Joy and Honey followed them. "I'm ready for a good meal. Are you?"

"I sure am. Do you want to leave Honey here with Playmate or shall we ride them over to the food concession?" Karen smiled. She was glad to have met a neat lady who just happened to be a lesbian and a horsewoman as well.

"Let's let the girls get acquainted while we do." Joy tied Honey's reins to the same post where Playmate was and she walked away with Karen.

Both horses whinnied at the women. Joy looked back. "I guess they don't like staying behind."

"Crazy girls," said Karen. "They've got grain and each other." In her heart, Karen thought to herself, "and we do too."

Like Karen, Joy was tall, slender, with a few silver strands in her dark hair, wearing western boots, jeans and long-sleeved shirts. Karen's western hat was of straw while Joy's appeared to be an old favorite made of felt.

They matched strides on their way to the food tent situated near the front gate.

After ordering the fried chicken platter and beer, they shared stories about their lives and horses.

"That was delicious, for fair food," said Karen as she finished her chicken. She sipped from her glass of beer, then laughed. "I've got to tell you what I read online this morning. It so fits this moment. It seems that a Boston hospital just received a million and a half dollars for the single purpose of studying why a higher percentage of lesbians are overweight than straight women. Can you believe that?" She laughed and Joy joined her.

"You've got to be kidding." Joy finished her beer. "How in the world did they come up with that statistic? What fat woman would ever tell some survey taker that she was a lesbian?" She started laughing again.

Karen joined her in the laughter. "It's true. The study was funded by the Eunice Kennedy Shriver Foundation, JFK's sister's foundation. Makes you wonder which of the Kennedy women might have been a closeted lesbian. Of course, that's what the religious right people will be saying. Doesn't mean it's true."

Karen shook her head. "What will they think of next?" She paused a moment. "I know. Another group was turned down on their request for money to find out why heterosexual males have twice as much obesity as gay males. Maybe they'll get funded next year." She could hardly talk through her laughter.

After their giggling session, the older women ordered pecan pie for dessert.

Karen rubbed her chin. "I was just thinking. We could probably solve both those so-called problems. Too many lesbians live alone with too few places to meet another lesbian any place other than a gay bar. They stay home alone every evening watching television and eating too much. On the other hand, most heterosexual men finish their workday, then go home to eat a big dinner cooked by their woman, and sit in front of the television drinking beer. My theories." She laughed.

"My dear Karen, you've just earned over a million dollars. Cases solved." Joy laughed with her. "Of course, they'll spend all that money to come up with the same answers."

"But, what are the solutions to the problems?" Karen ordered another beer for each of them.

"We have to drink this here so maybe we have time to solve the problems," Joy said as she sipped from her glass. "What lesbians need are more places to meet each other. The non-alcohol crowd needs more opportunities to meet. They are left out when the primary meeting place has always been the gay bar."

"I agree with that. Maybe with this new century when more gays feel they can be out, there will be more opportunities for the younger ones and for those who don't drink alcoholic beverages. Of course, that still leaves the born-again Christians in limbo; they can't be out at their church, and they won't go into bars. They're the ones living alone and lonely to avoid being ostracized. Surely they have to feel unhappy every day their hearts can't be with someone they can love. Statistics say more than seventy-eight percent of church-goers are anti-gay. There's no chance they'll give up their fiendish pleasure of hating gays. Damn them, anyway." Karen's anger was evident in the spirited tone of her voice.

"Karen, I wish you weren't correct. I wish there was the possibility they would change. As long as angry men are their leaders, church-goers will hold fast to their anger. And, as long as that happens, too many young gays will commit suicide." Joy shook her head. "I just don't understand it."

They finished their beer and walked back to Playmate and Honey.

Ending Everything

"You're out of time! Get out now! I've had enough!" Janie threw Margo's shoes and clothes out the door. She ran back to the bedroom and gathered another armload and rushed to throw them out with the other things. "Get out, Margo. I never want to see your face again. I've been too stupid letting you stay here after you hit me. But, never again!"

Margo was stunned. And, she was speechless for a moment, while she watched Janie throw another temper tantrum.

****

Janie had moved to San Francisco two years earlier to start a new job with a book publisher. As soon as she got settled into an apartment, she went to the gay bar in the neighborhood, sat at a table by herself and ordered her favorite drink. Sipping slowly, she observed all the people in the bar.

She wondered if there was a lesbian in Frisco who would like he Frisco.

She watched a tall, short haired woman with a cute smile walk in.

Unlike Janie, she wore blue denim jeans, a long-sleeved shirt with the cuffs rolled up, and walked, some would say, "like a tomboy."

Janie smiled at the woman and was surprised when the woman ordered a drink and walked to her table.

"Hi, I'm Margo. I haven't seen you here before."

Janie liked her smile. "I'm Janie. New from Sacramento."

"Janie. That's a sweet name. I like the way you've fixed your hair. The pageboy style is so feminine, and your blue eyes sparkle. I could see them when I was standing at the door. You're something else." Margo patted Janie's hand and grinned. "Gorgeous woman."

Janie was enthralled at Margo's compliments. She felt adored as she let Margo's words sink into her sense of who she was.

After talking a while, Margo asked, "Would you like to go to a movie? I want to see 'Argo' and it's showing at the Strand, just a short walk from here?" She put her arm around Janie's shoulder and pulled her close.

Janie liked having Margo's hand around her. "I'd love to."

Margo kissed Janie's cheek. "Let's go." Taking Janie's hand, she led her toward the door.

Janie enjoyed the romantic attention during the movie, and kept thinking just how good it was to be in the arms of somebody special.

After the movie, Margo walked Janie to her apartment. "Janie, it's been great. See you again tomorrow at happy Hour." She kissed Janie before leaving.

The following day the two women met at Happy Hour again, and stayed until after midnight before Margo walked Janie home again.

As she unlocked her door, Janie smiled and asked Margo, "Would you like to come in? We can share a glass of wine and watch a late show on television?" She hoped Margo would want to stay longer and maybe even make love to her for her first time.

"Sure." Margo went inside and Janie closed the door.

Janie handed Margo a glass of wine then went to the bathroom before sitting beside her.

Margo sipped from her glass and put her arm around Janie who looked into her eyes.

They kissed and Margo pulled Janie close. Janie pushed her breasts tightly against Margo's. Her insides trembled gently when their tongues played together in the kiss. She was awestruck as her passion increased until both of them were undressed and had shared sensual pleasures.

Janie looked into Margo's eyes. "My first time and it was wonderful."

"Honey, I loved making love to you. You're so hot, so beautiful. I'd love to do it every evening. What does that song say? 'Six times a week and twice on Sunday. Count them up, they come to eight." That's how often I'd like to make love to you."

Margo kissed Janie again before they slept together the remainder of the night.

The two of them spent the weekend just being together in Janie's apartment, eating, drinking wine, and passionate lovemaking.

By Monday, Margo had settled in to live with Janie. It seemed to happen without discussion or with Janie thinking through the matter. She had accepted a roommate, a sexual partner, not necessarily a committed, loving relationship.

Their first year together was happy for Janie; however, Margo changed.

Margo began to get drunk every weekend; then she started using marijuana, then heroin. She never had money to pay her share of the rent or utilities. She began to always be angry about something or someone. Often, she slapped Janie.

One weekend, Margo was so angry that she hit Janie over and over, leaving bruises and scratches on her body.

That scared Janie so badly, she made plans to be alone again. After sharing her fear with Lucille, her bartender, she decided to take her life back.

Having made her decision, one Saturday morning even before Margo was awake, Janie began to put everything that belonged to Margo, outside the apartment door.

Margo heard the noise and ran into the living room.

****

Janie railed. "This is my apartment. You have to leave. All your things are outside the door. You go too."

Margo laughed. "You can't kick me out. Not unless I want to leave."

Janie picked up the phone. "If you don't leave now, I'm calling the police. And, before you start anything again, just know that I've told Lucille how you've hurt me and she took photos of all the cuts and bruises. Your call? Or mine?" She started to dial 911.

"Stop. I'll leave." Margo started toward the door. "You ungrateful bitch. I'll get even some way. Just you wait."

She slammed the door on her way out.

Janie locked the door then she took a deep breath and blew it out slowly as she slumped into a chair.

"It's over. God, how did I allow all that to happen? Make me wise, God, and send me a sweet, kind sweetheart someday."

An Accidental Meeting

It was sunny and warm the day Karen Emerson hurried to her Chevy sedan and drove toward the sunset to Safeway.

The sun was blinding, but she felt sure she could see everything well enough to drive safely in crowded five o'clock traffic. She hadn't counted on a mother duck and her twelve ducklings march to the lake.

Suddenly the duck appeared with her ducklings walking in a straight line behind her, their heads up, crossing the street in front of Karen's sedan.

Karen yelled frantically while hitting the brake with high hopes of stopping before taking any causalities.

Bang! The sound of metal on metal filled the air.

The pickup behind her crashed into her bumper. Even so, Karen stopped before hitting a single duckling.

Breathing fast and hard, she watched cars in the opposite lane screech to a stop, in time for mother duck to safely take her ducklings for a late afternoon swim in the lake.

Karen leaned onto the steering wheel, thankful for her sudden stop for the duck's sake.

She got out of the car to see what damage had been done to her bumper; other drivers started blaring their horns to demand she get out of their way.

"Oh my gosh," she spoke fast with built-up nervous tension. "Your bumper's hung over mine. How can we release them and get out of this traffic?"

The woman from the red pickup looked at the situation. "I'm sorry, but you stopped so suddenly, I couldn't avoid hitting you." She climbed onto Karen's bumper and began to jump up and down until her bumper was freed. "It's left some scratches on your car. Let's pull over into the drug store's parking lot and exchange information so your car can get fixed." She hurried to get back in her pickup.

Karen starred at the damage, mute, and scratched her head, just standing there for several minutes. Other cars honked their horns again to demand she get her car out of her way.

Finally, Karen moved, got into her car and pulled forward to the parking lot.

The pickup parked beside her.

The woman who got out to talk to Karen, was wearing jeans, a Levi jacket and a western style straw hat; opposite to Karen in her sundress, that was low and showed plenty of her bountiful breast-line.

Karen looked at the woman and felt negative sensations sweep through her. She knew without a doubt that she was looking at a 'butch lesbian', a lesbian who was not as feminine as herself, a 'lipstick lesbian', was.

She knew she usually lost any argument with a 'butch lesbian' because they're so 'tomboyish' and strong in their ways and speech.

"I'm sorry, I shouldn't have stopped so suddenly, but I just couldn't hit the mama duck and her babies. They were so cute."

"It's a wonder all the other cars hadn't hit me, and each other.

"It was an accident that was the fault of the mama duck, not me or you. So, each of us should pay to fix our own car. Don't you agree?"

She took her hat off then bent over and looked closely at the damaged grill of her pickup, and the scratches on Karen's sedan.

Karen stammered, feeling intimidated by the stronger woman. She had no defense against Dorothy's comments.

She caved. "You're right. I'll take responsibility for fixing my paint job and you do the same for yours."

Dorothy grinned. "With that in mind, I guess we don't need to exchange the names of our insurance agents."

"Okay." Karen spoke timidly while looking at the asphalt of the parking lot. "I'm sorry. I wish I could have signaled in time for you to stop safely." Having taken full responsibility for the accident, she clinched her fists, wishing she had enough 'backbone' to stand up for herself.

A moment later she took two steps toward Dorothy, "No, it's your fault. The law always says it's the fault of the driver who was driving too close. I want your driver's license information and the name of your insurance agent."

Dorothy, who had started to get back inside her pickup, turned, took her wallet from the hip pocket of her jeans and handed it to Karen. "Here's my insurance agent's name." She smiled and waited while Karen got a pen from her car and wrote the information down.

When Karen finished copying the information, she smiled at Dorothy and handed her the license and card. "Thank you."

Dorothy held Karen's hand for a moment as she took her license and the insurance card. "Let's start over." She looked into Karen's eyes, "May I buy you a cup of coffee? I like the way you stood up for yourself. There's a café next to the drug store. Will you take time to join me and let's be friends?"

"Sure. I'd prefer that." Karen clicked her key chain to lock her sedan. "We can walk over."

Dorothy locked her pickup and took her place in step with Karen. "I guess I was a bit intimidating at first. I apologize. Too bad, we can't hold the mama duck responsible for the craziness of the moment." She laughed.

Karen laughed. "I hate myself for being that way. Supposedly, I learned from my last partner, a 'butch dyke' like you seem to be, that I should stand up for myself. She put me down so much, I almost lost myself. I wasn't that way when I fell in love with her. Darn it, I just folded when I saw you reminding me of her."

Dorothy put her hand on Karen's shoulder. "It's funny, hearing you say that because it's the very reason my last partner left me. She said I came on too strong, too intimidating. And, I've been trying to change and to be mellower. I hope you'll forgive me. I don't want to be that way anymore."

Karen smiled. "I knew I was right. I knew you had to be a lesbian; another strong dyke coming across my path." She paused a moment, and took Dorothy's hand in hers. "I was suddenly attracted to you, so acted, at first, like I thought you expected. I want to be strong enough not to be intimidated by the very type of lesbian I like the most." She laughed.

They walked into the café, sat at a booth and ordered coffee.

"I'm buying, Karen. I'm glad we've met."

"Thanks, Dorothy. Have you lived in Sacramento very long?"

"Yes, I graduated from high school here. You?"

Karen sipped her coffee. "I moved here last year after I was single again. I graduated from Livingston, a small town and school where I met Joan, my dyke partner. I work at Safeway as Credit Manager."

"I teach physical education at Martin Luther High School. Same school I graduated from eight years ago." Dorothy drank from her cup. "Luckily, lesbians can teach school now; so different from a few decades ago."

The two women shared conversation until their cups were empty, then walked back to their vehicles.

Before she got into her car, Karen asked, "Dorothy, let's bike through Central Park Saturday morning?" She smiled as she saw a smile cross Dorothy's face.

"Sure. Let's meet at the parking lot at the base of the California path. Do you know where that is?"

"Yes, I'll see you there, say at ten." Karen got into her car.

"Ten's good. I'll see you then." Dorothy went to her pickup.

They met on Saturday morning, took their bike ride, went dancing at the Rainbow bar that evening, and have been together as partners and lovers for two years.

Ann Patterson

118

A Tryin' Cryin' Time

When she heard the garage open, Sharon hurried to the kitchen to wash the whiskey from the glass, and then she took her Betty Crocker cookbook from the shelf, opened it and began turning the pages. She grabbed a few peppermints and chewed them. She knew there'd be 'hell to pay' if Marsha smelled the whiskey.

Marsha came in carrying a bag of groceries. "Hi Sweetie. Sorry I was gone so long." She turned to kiss Sharon.

"Dammit, Sharon. You lied to me. Not two hours ago, you said you weren't drinking; that there was no alcohol in the house." She slammed the bag to the floor.

Apples, potatoes and other things scattered across the kitchen. "I can smell it on you. It smells awful mixed with peppermints." She started opening cabinets and pushing things around the shelves, looking for the bottle. "Where is it?"

Sharon cowered back against the refrigerator. "I'm sorry, Honey. I started cooking dinner and came across an almost empty bottle. As I was pouring it in the sink, I just had to have a little." Sheepishly, she slowly reached to the back of the dishtowel drawer for the bottle, and handed it to Marsha. "I'm trying, but sometimes it gets the best of me."

Marsha took the bottle. "It's the lying more than the drinking. It's still got a few shots in it; so you lied again just now when you said you poured it in the sink."

She slammed her fist on the counter, breaking a saucer, "I hate the lying."

Holding her hand to stop the pain, she stared out the window.

Sharon wasn't afraid Marsha would hurt her, but she feared she'd leave her. "Marsha, I'm sorry; I'm trying. And I know I'm not there yet. I'm sorry I lied. I'm sorry." She turned away, crying, her shoulders shaking. "I hate this. I hate it."

Marsha stepped to her side and put her arm around Sharon's shoulders. "I know, Honey. I know you want to quit drinking, even more than I want you to. I love you and I want the best for us. You've just got to go to A.A. on a regular basis, and especially when you feel the urge to buy or drink."

Sharon turned into Marsha's arms and let her tears fall against her shirt.

Marsha held her close and kissed her just in front of her ear.

After Sharon calmed herself, she finished cooking dinner; then they went to the living room to eat while watching television.

Sharon and Marsha had met at Ellie's, a lesbian bar in Seattle during Gay Pride a year earlier. After a few weekend dates, Sharon had moved in with Marsha and their permanent relationship began. Sharon's alcohol consumption was "too much every day" while Marsha's pattern was to have a few drinks on the weekend.

As Sharon's drinking had increased, so had their troubles. She always said, "I'm tryin'. I'm always tryin' to stop."

Marsha ate slowly and Sharon ate very little. During the rest of the evening, the anger dissipated and they laughed together through the "Will and Grace" sitcom.

Sitting beside Sharon, Marsha began to stroke the back of her neck, then kissed her. "I do love you, my precious wife. And I want to always be with you." She continued the kiss, then lifted Sharon's shirt over her head, lay her down and began to caress her breasts, first with her hand, then with her lips.

Sharon, already relaxed from the alcohol, let her body absorb the tingling sensations from Marsha's lips, her tongue and the touch of her hand. A relaxed smile crossed her face as her body jerked when Marsha tousled her mound of curls, then the sensitive membranes beneath. "Oh, Honey, don't stop. Ohhh, that's so good." Her soft moans signaled her lover of the perfection of every touch and kiss.

Marsha's fingernails gently scraped against 'just-kissed' nipples, as she kissed a trail, pausing at her sweetheart's belly button, then alongside her soft curls.

Sharon's body moved slowly side to side, grasping every sensation, sweeping through her from Marsha's kissing and nibbling, inch by inch from the curls into sensitive wet membranes.

"Honey, ahhh, ohhh," her gentle sounds of pleasure increased; then suddenly she writhed with energy when Marsha's lips grabbed her sensitive spot, sucking and licking speedily until Sharon's climax passed.

"So nice," Sharon's soft voice was music to Marsha's ears, as her lover pulled her head toward her lips for a long, lingering kiss while she relaxed in the love.

Sharon whispered, "I love you, Marsha, so much."

Holding her wife close, their lips touching, Marsha responded, "And I love you. Now and forever."

They lay together on the sofa until both of them were asleep.

Bright sunlight beaming through the window awakened Sharon.

She watched Marsha open her eyes, then smiled, "Good morning. Did you rest?"

"Yes, Sweetheart. More importantly, did you? I'm still so relaxed from last night." Sharon kissed Marsha on her nose. "I want to love you like you love me." She picked up Marsha's hand and played with her fingers, "Honey, I want to always be good to you."

Marsha smiled. "I know. Honey, I know; and you will."

"I'm tryin'."

The following month went smoothly and for Marsha and Sharon.

Marsha credited the peace with the fact that Sharon went to A.A. meetings at noon and again after work. She would get home with positive thoughts learned from A.A. friends who, like her, were working every day to overcome the cries of their bodies and minds to consume alcohol, the poison that could kill them.

Marsha would listen with both her ears and heart to her wife whom she truly wanted in her life for the rest of her days.

"Sharon," Marsha called her from the kitchen. "Let's go camping this weekend. It's the Fourth of July and we get an extra day. I'd love to go to that campground by the beach. What do you think?"

She took fried chicken from the skillet and placed it on the table.

Sharon appeared at the door of the kitchen. "I'd love to. We can leave right after work Friday."

She sat at her end of the table. "Honey, this looks wonderful. You're such a good cook."

Marsha kissed Sharon before she sat down to eat. "Let's go to Mossyrock so we can catch some fish for one of our meals. Our camper's still packed with everything except us and the food."

"Sounds perfect to me. And, I promise it won't be like last fall when I got so drunk and made a fool of myself. I want it to be a happy weekend for both of us." Sharon served herself her favorite piece of the fried chicken. "Oh, do I love the breast."

Marsha giggled. "I know you do and not just the one on your plate." She winked.

"Yes, Sweetheart, and yours are so perfect." Sharon giggled. "Maybe I can nuzzle them a little later. Hmmm."

Sharon laughed. "Hold that thought."

The week passed quickly and they hooked the camper to their station wagon to drive to Mossyrock, south of Seattle on Highway 12 West. It was dark by the time the camper was set-up and a warm fire was burning. Sharon cooked a quick meal while Marsha sat by the fire enjoying its warmth.

As soon as she could, Sharon sat in her chair beside Marsha. "This is heaven. Just you and me and the camper. I'm feeling really good right now; no desire for anything but this peaceful setting and you."

"It means so much to me for you to feel so good. You complexion is prettier, you eyes are clear and bright, you're losing the pounds you wanted to, and we have good and peaceful times together. Sobriety is wonderful. Keep it up."

Marsha pursed her lips to send a kiss to Sharon.

"It's still so hard every evening to keep my mind off of gin and tonic. Even so, I keep working toward our goal. I'll make it, Honey. Trust me." Sharon set her plate aside and drank her coke.

"Please don't say 'trust me' when talking about drinking. I heard that a thousand times when you were still sneaking a drink. I love you, but trusting you when it's been about alcohol, has been the most difficult thing for me." Marsha picked up their empty plates then went to the camp table to wash them.

Sharon helped put things away for the night. "It's just too odd, putting the food and such in this big steel container so the bears and cougars don't get to it, while at the same time, most campers here are sleeping in a cloth tent." She put her hand on her hip and added, "I guess the bears don't eat people, just the food people eat. Doesn't make sense." She sat at the table across from Marsha, still laughing.

Marsh laughed with her. "Makes me glad we have a camper instead of a tent."

After the food and dishes were put away, the couple sat near the campfire, relaxing until the flames turned to red embers, then they went into the camper for the night.

"Good Boy, Wolf"

"Wolf! Wolf boy! Wolf! Where are you?" Lily Kale called for the wolf pup she loved and had trained to be gentle and kind, except when someone was threatening. Then, his grumpy growl would win the day.

It was a perfect love Wolf and Lily shared with Marnie Kendal, her sweetheart. The family of three lived on a homestead forty miles outside of Anchorage, Alaska.

Lily kept calling. "Wolf! Wolf boy! Come, baby!" Her voice softened as she finished calling because she saw Wolf running from the forest surrounding their house.

She knelt to receive him with hugs and kisses, and to endure the happy licks on her face. "Come on, boy. It's time to be inside for the night."

Panting in loud whispers, Wolf walked beside Lily to the door, then inside with her. "Marnie, Wolf's in. He was out in the woods again. I guess he's looking for rabbits or field mice." He laughed. "You know he likes those more than the healthy food you feed him."

Marnie stood in the doorway to the kitchen. "You're right; but he still needs the vitamins and minerals in the food I give him." She knelt. "Come, Wolf, give mommy a kiss. Good boy." When Wolf finished licking her face and enjoying her hugs, she turned to Lily, "Dinner's ready."

While Lily and Marnie ate pork chops, potatoes, gravy and green beans for dinner, Wolf crunched his dry dog food then sat by the table between his pets that were called "mommy".

He went to sleep.

"Lily, I was just listening to the news on the radio. Great Britain has approved gay marriage. We're in the wrong country this year. America has focused on constitutional rights for our citizens far longer than Britain has; we should have been ahead of them for marriage equality." Marnie sipped from her coffee cup.

After spreading butter on her bread, Lily said, "I agree. But America isn't too far behind. In the last two years there've been major changes here. Now, fifty eight percent of Americans agree that gays and lesbians should have all marriage rights, both state and federal. I think it will happen before you and I grow old and die."

Lily looked into Marnie's eyes. "Honey, I want it to happen soon. I'm closer to sixty-five than you are. If I die first, I want you to have access to my Social Security payments. If we're married under the laws of the state and country, life will be better for the one who survives." Lily cut her salmon into bite sizes and put a piece on her fork. "We've paid taxes of every kind so we should have equal rights to such benefits."

Marnie described the details of the news report. "The news played the short speech of David Lammey in Parliament, who said, 'separate but equal is a fraud'. He reminded his fellow lawmakers that "separate but equal" was the language that tried to push Rosa Parks to the back of the bus, then he went on to name other American injustices of the segregationists and the racists. He was powerful when he said that for the law to not recognize full equality, that the country 'allows the rot of homophobia to fester' against homosexual men who love men and lesbian women who love women. They debated for six hours, then voted to agree with him."

Lily remembered something she had read. "Oscar Wilde spent years in prison 'for loving men too much.' While in prison, he wrote something like, 'society offers no place for me; but 'Nature whose sweet rains fall on the unjust and just alike, will hide me so that I may weep undisturbed.' It was a powerful statement. I wish I could remember all he wrote. Thank God, today we don't go to prison because we love each other."

Lily smiled and took Marnie's hand. "I love you so much."

****

Marnie met Lily fourteen years earlier in Seattle. Separately, they had gone to the Bistro, a new gay bar there, and happened to sit at the same large cocktail table.

Marnie was at a table, looking beautiful with her long blond hair, brown eyes and a winning smile. Her make-up had been deftly applied, giving her femininity special beauty.

She wore a yellow sundress, bare at the shoulders where thin straps held her dress in place and allowed the gentle cleavage to show.

Two other lesbians were sitting with her.

Lily walked in, looked around, and then went to the table where Marnie was sitting. Standing behind the other women, she put her hands on their shoulders and asked, "Hi, Grace and Judy. Mind if I sit with you, or are you waiting for someone else?"

One of them answered, "Sure, Lily."

Grace waved her hand toward Marnie, "Meet Lily. She's new in Seattle. Lily, this is Marnie, she's not as fierce as she looks." She laughed.

"Hi, Lily. Don't believe Grace. I'm not that fierce. The best I could do would be to kill a bear with my bare hands." She laughed and held her hands out. "Most of the time, these are gentle, loving hands." She pretended she was going to strangle Grace; everyone laughed.

Marnie watched Lily slide onto the seat beside her. "It's good to meet you, Marnie. Grace and Judy have been my friends for years."

Lily took her wallet from her pants' pocket. "I see your glass is empty. May I buy you a drink?"

Marnie smiled. "Thanks. I love your name. It speaks of a soft, gentle person who befriends children and other good people."

"Wow!" Lily laughed. "I like that."

Marnie smiled. She looked into Lily's deep blue eyes and saw something special. Lily's brown hair was short and wavy; she was wearing black pants with a white dress shirt and a red sport's coat. Marnie grinned when she saw Lily was wearing western boots. Her eyes met Lily's and a soft smile crossed Lily's face. A soft tingling sensation seemed to sweep through her.

"So, Marnie, where'd you come from? Seattle's a gathering place for gay guys and lesbians. That's why I moved here from Montana a couple of years ago." Lily paid for their drinks and took a sip.

"Same reason I just moved from Idaho. As soon as I got a job lined up, I loaded the U-haul truck and was on my way. I started my job last Monday." Marnie lifted her glass toward Lily. "To the future."

Grace and Judy joined the toast and lifted their glasses toward Lily and Marnie before the four happy, loving lesbians drank together.

From that evening, Lily and Marnie have been together.

In 2001, they gave up their jobs, took their savings, and moved to Alaska where they homesteaded. Both of them have worked in Anchorage during the week with weekend time to enjoy their homestead and Wolf, the wolf cub who has become their 'beloved child'. By living in the rural area, they have enjoyed privacy while hoping to keep their lesbian relationship, as if they're married, a secret from the hateful people in the world.

****

After dinner, Marnie and Lily washed the dishes, then sat at the table to play Checkers.

Wolf was dozing by the fireplace.

He growled then walked toward the door, his head down and his body low with his legs bent as though he was ready to pounce.

He continued to growl.

Lily rushed to the hall and took her loaded shotgun from the gun rack.

She gave Marnie the pistol. "Hide behind the sofa. If it's not someone we know, at least they won't see you at first."

Marnie went to her knees between the sofa and the wall.

Wolf continued to growl as he moved to stand beside Lily, still ready to pounce if given the signal from her. She knew he would pounce even without a signal if someone tried to hurt her.

The sounds of a fist hammering on the door scared Lily.

She stood still, and waited.

A man's voice yelled, "Open the door, you bitches! We're here for some fun!" Without further warning, the door was kicked in, and two men started into the room.

"Hut!" Lily yelled as she pointed her gun, hoping to stop the men.

Wolf knew Lily had told him to attack. He hit full body against the first man's chest, knocking him to the floor.

Lily saw a pistol in the other man's hand. She pulled the trigger of her shotgun.

Wolf held his open mouth at the throat of the one man.

Lily ignored the dead body at her feet, ran to the gun rack and grabbed a rope she kept there for any kind of emergency.

Marnie came out from behind the couch, and pointed her gun at the man's head. "If Wolf doesn't chew your head off, I'll blow your brains out."

Lily tied the rope, first to one of the villain's ankle, then to the other; then tied both together. "Roll over and put your hands together."

He grumbled. "No, that wolf will kill me."

His eyes were bulging in fear.

"Roll over very slowly and he'll not hurt you. Move fast and he'll gnaw your head off." Lily watched him roll over and hold his hands together.

While Wolf kept his open mouth at the man's neck, Marnie held the pistol with both shaking hands while Lily tied his hands behind the man's back."

"Keep quiet and Wolf won't bite. Stay very still." Lily took the pistol from Marnie. "I'll watch him while you go to the truck and radio the Sheriff."

The Sheriff and a deputy arrived in their van so they could take both the prisoner and the dead body back to town.

After getting all necessary information, he told Lily and Marnie, "Lucky ladies. Wolf and you could have been hurt. I'm glad to know you can take care of yourselves. Let me know, whenever you think anyone is a danger to you. You're good people, and as far as I'm concerned, you have every right everyone else in my county does."

He patted Wolf's head.

"I had heard you two had a wolf cub out here. I'm glad to see you've trained him well." He knelt down to look into Wolf's eyes. "Good boy. You're a good boy, Wolf."

Wolf licked his hand. Then the Sheriff left.

Marnie and Lily hugged each other close for several minutes, then kissed before getting busy cleaning the floor, and putting their home back in order. Then they sat on the sofa with Wolf between them.

"If I can't have you..."

There was a loud banging on the front door.

Amy stirred, but feeling drowsy, she closed her eyes again, responding to her need for sleep. She didn't know what had awakened her.

"Slam! Bang!" The front door rattled. Amy jumped up and hurried to find out who was banging on the door.

"Amy! Amy! Open the door! Open it now!" Charlotte Rangen yelled. She knew Amy was home and was determined to talk to her.

She saw a light go on and thought it was from the hallway. Amy was awake and should be at the door any minute. "Amy! I know you're home." Damn you! We've got a thing to settle! Let me in!"

Amy heard Charlotte's voice; she didn't dare open the door.

She grabbed the telephone and dialed 911. "Send the police. Someone wants to kill me. She's Charlotte Rangen and is banging my door down. Hurry. I'm scared."

Amy's hands were shaking and cold chills rushed over her skin. Her voice quivered, "It's Charlotte Rangen. If I'm found dead, you know she got in before the police." She ran to the bathroom and locked the door.

"Amy! Open this door!" Charlotte hit the door so hard, she hurt her hand. "Damn. I've broken it. I'll break her neck." She ran around to the side of the small house and grabbed a flower pot, threw it through the window and started removing glass shards so she could climb in.

Amy closed the lid on the commode and sat down. Still on the phone with the 911 operator, she said, "I just heard a window break. She's coming in. She'll kill me." Tears were streaming down her face and her fear was like a paralysis.

Holding her damaged hand close to her belly, Charlotte pulled herself up and through the window with her good hand. "Ouch," she cut her head on the sharp piece of glass above her. It started bleeding profusely as scalp cuts always do. Wiping the blood, streaming down her forehead, she headed down the hall. The bedroom doors were open and the bathroom door was closed.

"I'm coming, Amy. Nobody leaves me like you did. Now that I've found you, you're mine forever!" She kicked at the door, but lost her balance and fell.

"Operator, she's kicking the door down. Where're the cops?" Her voice cracked into a whisper. "She'll kill me just because I left her months ago in Selma, Alabama. I never believed she'd find me." Amy looked up at the small window and wished she could climb through it.

Again, Charlotte kicked at the door. The door opened. She grinned and shouted. "I told you what I'd do if you ever left me. You're mine, girl. You're mine." She knocked the phone from Amy's hand, leaving her own blood on Amy's face.

Amy ducked, then tried to run past Charlotte. She bumped into Charlotte's injured hand.

"Owww! You bitch!" Charlotte grabbed Amy by her long red hair. "You won't get away. If I can't have you, nobody can." She turned Amy's face upward, toward her own and bent to kiss her."

Amy tried to turn her face away from Charlotte's, but Charlotte's lips grabbed hers and wouldn't let go.

She quit struggling.

Suddenly the front door was broken by the police who rushed in with guns in their hands. They rushed toward the hall where they could see the bathroom door was open.

Charlotte knew the police were in. She kissed Amy harder and deeper with her tongue while holding her in place by her hair. "You're mine. I didn't want you to leave. I love you Amy."

Blood spilled from her head to Amy's.

Two policemen held their guns on the women as one stepped into the bathroom. "Let her go. Get your hands on top of your head."

Charlotte kissed Amy again, then stood up, turned and faced the policeman while putting her good hand on her head. "Okay. Okay. She's mine. You're mine forever, Amy." She held her injured hand at her waist.

One policeman handcuffed Charlotte, while the other helped Amy get up from the floor.

"It's her blood, not mine," groaned Amy as she gently touched her scalp where Charlotte's pulling her hair was still hurting."

"Thank you. I thought I was going to die. Thank you."

Both women were taken to hospitals, two different medical centers, for the help they needed. Boston police officers went with each of them to document their stories.

****

Two years earlier, Amy King was sitting at the Silence, the only gay bar in Selma, Alabama. The owner, Mark Freeport, had purchased the bar in the 1980's, renamed it, and it has been a bar for gay men and lesbians since that time.

There had been critical events there many times, either raids by the police or fighting and trouble started by angry heterosexuals who wanted the police to close down the bar. Somehow, Mark had managed to keep the bar open, even though the place was closed down many times by the police when the hate-filled straights created problems while trying to close the business permanently.

Now the general area of Selma and police ignored the bar. Mark was grateful that the times and attitudes were changing, though slowly.

Amy had stopped for Happy Hour after her day's work at the Power Company. She was the only redheaded woman in the Silence that day, and the only person wearing a work shirt with the logo of the Power Company on it, jeans and cowboy boots. She was drinking a whiskey sour.

"That's a pretty strong drink for a woman," said the lady who had just sat down beside her.

Amy turned to see who was speaking. "Tells you I'm a pretty strong woman." Amy laughed.

"Emphasize the 'pretty'." The woman with short blond hair combed back on both sides, wearing a checkered shirt and jeans, smiled and added, "Hi. I'm Charlotte."

"Amy King. Glad to meet you, Charlotte."

Mark stopped to take her order. "A gin and tonic for me and another whiskey sour for her," Charlotte ordered.

"Thanks," said Amy. "Two's my limit. I've learned not to have a third one until I've eaten." She finished emptying her glass.

Charlotte smiled. "You look to me about my age. I'm twenty-one, just had my first legal drink at Christmas 1998. So I'm still celebrating being legal." She laughed.

"A lady never tells her age, so you've got my silence." Amy reached for the drink Mark had set in front of her while Charlotte handed him her credit card.

"Amy, I'd like to buy dinner for you, here or wherever you choose; since you won't have another drink until you eat. Also, I hope you'll stick around for tonight's Drag Show."

"They have a Drag Show here? I didn't know. This is my first time at the Silence since I moved to Selma." Amy smiled. "Sure, I'll have dinner with you and would love to see the Drag Show."

****

After doctors checked Amy for injuries, the police officer sat in the Emergency Room with her. "How did you know Charlotte?"

Amy trembled. "We met in Selma. When we first moved in together, everything was calm until Charlotte began to get 'mean drunk' every single day. I guess all the drinking put her in the frame of mind her alcoholic father was when he abused her and his whole family. I saved money on the side; then one day I boarded a train instead of going to work. I haven't seen her since then. That was in January 2000. I never expected to see her again; until tonight, and you know how that went."

"She's being treated elsewhere, will be arrested and tried for the various crimes of this evening. It's important that you not visit her, and that you remain available for any further contacts the detectives wish to make with you." The officer looked over the form to be sure she had gathered all required details. "Is there anyone you need to call? Your home has a broken front door and window, so you may want to stay elsewhere the rest of the night."

"I'll go to the Super Eight. I'll feel safe there and won't go to work tomorrow. I do need a ride though."

Amy had become calmer after her conversation with the officer. "I have my wallet with me so I'll be okay otherwise."

From the Locker Room

Coach Margo Locklear pointed toward her forward, her piece of chalk in her hand. "Julie, if you complete the play I've just showed you, we'll win the Championship."

She waved her hand across the whole soccer team in front of her. "Julie can only do that if each of you carries out your part of the play; as planned!"

She put the chalk in the tray below the blackboard. "Got it?"

In one voice, the team shouted, "Got it, Coach!'

The team shouted with the roaring crowd as they ran from the locker room to the field. Determination filled their hearts as they faced the University of Tennessee for the final quarter of the nation's women's soccer season.

Coach Margo had every confidence in Julie; not just for the game, but for the remainder of their lives off the field.

****

Margo was twenty-seven when she landed the position of Women's Soccer Coach at the university. She was beautiful, single and had proven herself a master at the game during her years in college, and subsequently, as assistant coach to her mentor. The job became hers after cancer had taken the life of her mentor. She was the youngest among the Head Coaches of the nation's university soccer teams.

It was also the first year Julie Mandel was on the team.

Julie, twenty years of age, was tall with long curls, worn as a ponytail on the soccer field, grew up in a small rural town in rural Kansas where she was an all-around sports woman with awards in soccer.

Margo had recruited Julie to play for the University of Southern Baptists in eastern Kansas.

They first met at Julie's home when Margo visited with her family to make her recruitment proposal. Julie's conservative, middle class family was overjoyed at the offer so Julie became Margo's star player immediately.

The relationship between the two women quickly became something more than friends, beyond just 'coach and player'. It was at a time when neither of them was out as a lesbian to anyone in their circles.

Julie moved into her dorm room on a Sunday, three weeks before class was scheduled to begin. That evening she went to the mall to buy some new clothes.

While Julie was selecting a dress outfit, she looked up and saw Margo standing across from her, also selecting an outfit. "Hello, Coach Margo." She smiled.

Margo smiled. "Julie, it's wonderful meeting you here. You're the first team member in town." She carried a matching outfit with her as she walked closer to Julie. "Today, just call me Margo; we're not at the university."

"Okay, Margo. We're almost the same age so I can do that." She laughed. "My parents always taught me to include titles when talking to adults."

"Sweetie, you're an adult also. Are you getting the blue one or the green outfit?" Margo had presented herself as a friend and equal to Julie, not as a superior. She smiled as she waited for Julie to make her choice of outfits.

From the moment she had first met Julie, her heart was warmed in a special way, unlike toward any other girl or woman she had known. It reminded her of the crush she had on Jean Baxter in her high school freshman year and of her disappointment when Jean started going steady with Mike Baldwin.

At Julie's home that day, she remembered, she almost changed her mind about recruiting Julie with a hope she could one day recruit love from her heart for them to share.

Julie interrupted Margo's thoughts. "I'll take the blue one; our school colors, you know." She carried the outfit to the cashier and paid for it.

Julie waited as Margo paid for her purchase. "I'm headed somewhere for dinner. Where's a good place to eat around here?"

"Why don't you join me? I'm going to the Country Steakhouse, down the block from the mall." Margo smiled and brushed her reddish auburn hair away from her eye.

"Sounds good. I'd like that." Julie stepped to Margo's side and they exited the mall. "I don't know anybody in town yet. I think it's great to be with a friend this evening." Julie was already feeling a special friendship with Margo. She knew herself to be a lesbian and how it felt to have a crush on a beautiful girlfriend. Those same feelings were in her heart that moment. She wondered if it was because Margo was her coach, or was it something more; would be nice if it was.

They sat in a booth in the corner of the busy Steakhouse and ordered. Coffee was served right away to both women.

Margo sipped from her cup. "Julie, where did you grow up?" She didn't want their conversation to be about the university or the team, but something more personal.

Julie smiled. She was glad Margo hadn't asked about the university; she preferred normal conversation like she'd be having with a girlfriend. "I went to Blue Springs schools. My parents were farm people then; so I had lots of chores from early on. When I was older, I drove Daddy's tractor and plowed the fields. It was a good place to become who I am today, just a country girl who's had the privilege of going to college." She sipped her coffee.

"Same for me, a small town girl. I grew up in Iowa, a community south of DesMoines. My parents taught school there." Margo thanked the waitress who delivered their food.

By the time they ordered dessert, Julie and Margo were both comfortable with each other. Nobody in the restaurant had paid any attention to them.

After a taste of her apple pie, Julie looked into Margo's eyes. "I have a question of a personal nature, Margo. Do you know where there's a gay bar here? I don't want everyone to know; but I'm a lesbian and thought that might be a good place to meet friends I won't meet at the university. I hope you'll keep my secret." She looked down at her pie.

"No problem, Julie. I have the same secret. If you'd like, we can go there when we leave here. Our secret, of course." Margo's heart leaped inside her. She felt a level of joy that her new friend shared the most important part of her life.

Together, they went to the Insight where they shared time and nonalcoholic drinks, not just that afternoon, but periodically during the following two years.

They fell in love but managed to keep their relationship a secret during Julie's final two years of college, both on and off the soccer field.

****

The final moment of the championship game, the play was executed perfectly with the ball kicked to Julie, then with one great kick, it sailed past the goalie. Her team had won. She was carried off the field as the game's hero.

Graduation ceremonies were held the following Sunday afternoon.

Julie's parents spent the remainder of the afternoon with her at the dorm, then drove away, leaving her with a used Ford station wagon as her graduation gift. She packed everything from her room into the Ford and drove to her lover's home on the outskirts of town.

Margo opened the door to see Julie, a winning smile as her welcome.

Once inside, Julie and Margo shared a long, slow kiss.

Julie breathed a sigh. "Now we can really be together. I'm so happy."

Margo brushed a curl from Julie's face. "Yes, my sweet love, we're free to love each other now." She kissed her again, then took Julie's hand and led her to the kitchen where the table was set with candles and roses. "We have so much to celebrate and love to share."

After the dinner by candlelight, they sat together on the patio of Margo's ranch house for a while to enjoy a glass of wine and their bond of friendship, now one of romance and love.

The moon was bright and the night filled with stars. From nearby ranches, they could hear the whinny of horses, the mooing of cows and hooting of owls.

The air was cool and fresh, not like the stuffy air in town and the college crowd. It was a peaceful evening.

Margo got up and reached for Julie's hand. "Sweetheart, will you join me for our first night together in our bed?" She had not allowed herself the freedom of making love to Julie all the months of their two years at the university. In that moment, she felt joy swell her heart because they were free to be lovers in the most beautiful way.

Julie took Margo's hand and kissed her. "It's been so long while we've waited. Now, my sweetheart, we can truly be together. I'm very happy."

Margo flipped off the light switches as they walked to the bedroom, where she turned to kiss Julie as each of them removed clothing.

After the kiss, Margo grinned, "To the shower."

Julie laughed. "To the shower. I've heard you say that a thousand times; now I'm excited to go to the shower."

Under the spray of warm water, the lovers became acquainted with each other, body and soul, for the first time. As their passion intensified, they moved to the bed where they enjoyed love's fulfillment, sensually and physically for the first time.

A Time for Love

"I'm going to make you very happy," Tonya said to Mary before she kissed her. Then the two women turned to their family and friends, and smiled before walking up the aisle as wife and wife.

The crowd followed them and cheered as they watched the happy couple drive away for their honeymoon.

The sun was shining, the blue of the sky and the green of the shrubs and pastures looked brighter than ever, while Tonya drove to the Washington seashore to celebrate being married to the lovely woman at her side with eyes of blue.

Suddenly the sports car ahead of them had a blowout, and spun around facing Tonya. She couldn't avoid the crash.

****

Tonya had been celebrating her thirty-seventh birthday at the Blue Parrot when she saw a woman pause at the door before taking a seat at the bar. Tonya was stricken; her heart jumped and squeezed a message she couldn't ignore. Never had she seen so much beauty in one woman.

For a moment Tonya watched her desired heart-throb, then she picked up her drink and walked over. She stood by the barstool with a broad smile admiring the sandy long hair and the perfectly slender neckline, then she sat down, propped her head on her hand and starred, until the model of beauty looked into her eyes and smiled, "Hi."

"Hi, beautiful woman." Tonya set her drink down, got her credit card out and handed it to the bartender. "Her drink's on me and I'll take another."

"I'm Mary Kelton. I'm new here." Mary's eyes beamed as she smiled.

Tonya saw dimples decorate Mary's face. "I'm Tonya Nielson. I'm glad you're here."

The bartender set their drinks in front of them. Mary and Tonya took drinks in hand and sipped. The bartender saw how stricken Tonya was with the new girl, and grinned as she winked at Tonya.

Mary looked at her drink and saw it was shaking. Her nervousness was unusual for her. She took note of her beating heart almost jumping out of her chest. "I moved to Portland from Payette, Idaho, the little town across the border where they hate lesbians." She swept her curls away from her eye and looked up at Tonya. "I came here to feel free and be out among new friends."

"Mary, you're in the right place. I'm sorry if I've overwhelmed you, I didn't intend to. You'll find many friends here, not just at the Parrot, but even at work. The gay community is treated quite well here; no problems with the police and such, even though bigots live in Portland too."

Tonya was five feet, eight inches, one of the tallest women who partied at the Parrot. Her long red hair and emerald eyes set her apart. She had a soft, gentle voice as a 'soft butch' girl who didn't own a dress, just jeans and pant suits. A few freckles across her nose and her red lips drew attention to how beautiful she was. Still single in her thirties, she was popular, but always told friends she just hadn't met the right woman with whom to spend the rest of her life. Her approach to Mary actually was out of character for the fun-loving lesbian.

Mary looked around. The Parrot was crowded with women, and she loved listening to their voices. Since she had decided to come out as a lesbian, a bit late at the age of thirty-five, she was hungry for relationships with women, women not being led around in life by a man on her arm. The voices were music to her ears. She smiled when seeing two of them share a slow gentle kiss.

"Tonya, what's there to do in Portland besides coming to the Blue Parrot? And, where's the parrot? There must be one, hence the name." Mary's smile answered Tonya's.

"Well, we have a Drag Show here tonight; the only guys who come here are performers. Portland has wonderful Drag Queens to entertain us. Daytime when you're not at work, there're many parks, the zoo, fishing, boating, and a myriad of things to do. I hope you'll stay for the Drag Show tonight. I'll tell you what great guys they are when not in Drag."

Tonya sipped her drink.

"That, I'll do. I'll want to go somewhere to eat before it starts." Mary emptied her drink and waved toward the bartender as she set the empty glass near the far edge of the bar.

"I'll take you to Hobo's. It's an upscale bar with great dining and there's pool in the back. Do you play pool?"

"Yes, I'm pretty good at it." Mary laughed. "Of course, you may beat the socks off me."

"I doubt that. And, yes, Martha did have a blue parrot. It was killed last year when some of the bigots came in a started a brawl. One of them killed the parrot. All of them got jail sentences for their bigotry. Two were women."

Tonya's voice was sad as she spoke of the hurtful evening for Portland's lesbians.

After finishing their drinks again, Tonya led Mary to Hobo's where they ordered dinner.

"Thanks, Tonya, for bringing me here. It's a great place. It's nice to see families here along with gay couples and lesbians. I haven't told you, but I got a job before moving here. I've worked for Albertson's in Ontario for seven years, so I was able to have a job here without losing any of my benefits."

"That's great, Mary. I'm with the Power Company as Credit Manager. It's a good job. Keeps me happy and now I'm buying my own home. No more apartment living."

Tonya sipped from her water glass before turning her attention back to her salmon steak.

"I'm in a small apartment. It works for me."

When they finished eating, Tonya and Mary went to the pool room to challenge each other.

"Tonya, we're a good match. A game each. This has been fun." Mary put her cue stick in the rack and put her sweater back on.

The two new friends walked into the night air. Tonya took Mary's hand in hers and pointed out the gay bars as she described their entertainment and history. The gay area of Portland was part of China Town and Old Town, the area that had been upgraded by the City during recent decades. It was a safe place for individuals and gay couples to walk without hearing caustic remarks.

"Mary, let's go here for tonight's Drag Show. Bolivia Carmichael's the Drag Queen on Friday nights. She's a one woman show and the best there is. In daily life Bolivia's a sweet young man named Daniel, a friend to everyone he meets."

The walked into a wall to wall crowd at C.C. Slaughter's and sat together at a cocktail table that had just emptied near the dance floor.

While Bolivia performed in Drag, Tonya put her arm around Mary and pulled her close. She knew she had found her 'dream woman' in Mary. Her heart was warmed and special feelings swept through her heart, as she gently played her fingers against Mary's shoulder.

Mary laughed with Tonya at Bolivia's comedy. Together they went forward to tip the gorgeous blond Queen who teased Mary by not taking the dollar in her hand, but opened her bosom for Mary to drop the dollar inside. Mary blushed and laughed.

After the show, they walked toward the Blue Parrot where their cars were parked.

"Here's my car." Mary stopped at a blue Camry sedan.

Tonya turned to face Mary. "I don't want to say good-night to you. I've never felt so many wonderful feelings as I have being with you, Mary." She kissed her. "Will you go home with me tonight?"

Mary smiled, "I'd love to."

****

The car rolled and finally came to a stop. Tonya was penned by the steering wheel.

She could see her beautiful Mary, her precious wife, had not survived. Her body was in the seat but her head had broken through the side window.

Tonya cried out, both in pain and at seeing her sweet Mary destroyed so badly. She went unconscious.

Her days in the hospital were long and sad. She spent her waking moments in grief as she thought of Mary and her life ahead without her.

Days later, Tonya left the hospital. Her physical injuries were healing, but her broken heart might never heal.

Thankful she and Mary were married, Tonya arranged burial services for her wife. The five years they had together before moving to Washington to marry, were filled with wonderful memories and happy times. They had never been apart a single night after meeting until that horrible accident.

Supported by friends during her grief and convalesce, Tonya adjusted to being alone again. Her broken heart never expected to love anyone again, not the way she had loved Mary.

Rodeo Gals

Jill rode her horse in the rodeo every year. In recent years she had been the fastest and best when riding Cameo around the barrels, but her latest competitions were harder and harder to win. Competition had improved and she worried she might be bested in the Rodeo Finals by Shannon Wilson and her horse.

Jill didn't notice a woman standing behind her that evening at the Blackjack table in Reno. Her focus was on winning hand after hand as the cards were dealt. She didn't notice when the woman sat down until she put her money on the table because she had pulled her red cowboy hat down to cover her face so she could focus on the Ace and ten in her hand.

With a grin, she laid the cards down, face up.

"Way to go," said the woman beside her.

Jill removed her hat and looked into the deep blue eyes of the new player at the table. "Thanks." She was mesmerized by those eyes.

"Good to see you, Jill. You know me, I'm Shannon from Oklahoma."

"Right. You have the gorgeous pinto. Glad to meet you. We don't always get to meet anywhere other than the arena. I won last year, but you and the pinto are going to be hard to beat this year." Jill looked at the cards dealt to her, an Ace and a two, thirteen, a terrible hand. Would luck give her an eight, she wondered.

Shannon turned over an Ace and a Queen for a big win. "Wow, how'd that happen?"

Jill held her breath. She didn't dare look into those blue eyes again or she knew, she'd lose her concentration. She scraped her thirteen against the green felt on the table, hoping for an eight; she got a two. She gritted her teeth and said a prayer as she scraped the felt again. A six landed by her hand. "Thank you, God."

She picked up the card, looked at Shannon and into those deep blue eyes. "Thank you, Girl. You've kept me winning." She smiled as her heart skipped a beat; not for the card but the bit of sweetness in those blue eyes.

Jill and Shannon played a few more hands before the cards turned against them. At the same moment each of them slid off the stool to walk away.

"Let's have a drink, Shannon," Jill put her red hat as a crown for her long, wavy hair.

"Glad to, I've wanted to get to know you, Jill." Shannon put her hand on Jill's shoulder as they walked through the casino crowd.

Jill smiled. She enjoyed the warm hand guiding her toward the bar. Her feelings were stirring inside with a special joy, knowing she'd get to look into those blue eyes again over a drink, maybe even more.

The lovely waitress served drinks to Jill and Shannon. For a few moments, neither spoke; they just sipped from their glasses and looked into each other's eyes.

Jill put her hand on Shannon's. "I'm taken by your eyes. I don't think I've ever been so mesmerized by such gorgeous blues." She laughed, 'And, yes, I'm flirting with you."

Shannon smiled. "Why do you think I sat at the Blackjack table beside you? For the same reason. I've met a lot of pretty ladies, but no other has touched my heart like you have. Yesterday, in the arena I was wondering how I could get close to you. Jill, it's like love at first sight." She laughed. "If I'm out of line, tell me, but my heart tells me you're like me, a girl looking for a special girl to love." She winked.

"You're right, Shannon. I've been looking for love but not from guys. My heart's jumping around right now. I feel foolish, but..." Before Jill could finish her sentence, Shannon kissed her soft red lips.

"I couldn't resist. Jill, I've never done that before; not kissed a beautiful woman the first moment we're together. You're the one." Shannon straightened her blue felt hat.

"I'm glad you did. Your eyes drew me in and I wanted your kiss." Jill sipped from her drink then looked over her glass. "My head's spinning and I know it's not the gin."

Shannon nodded. "Mine too." She finished her drink.

Jill emptied her glass. "I hope you'll go to my room with me." She stood up and offered her hand to Shannon.

"My pleasure, my joy." Shannon took Jill's hand and they walked down the hall together.

They went inside Jill's room where she poured glasses of wine and they sat on the balcony.

"Jill, tell me about your Cameo. How long have you had her?"

"From the day she was born on my grandfather's farm. I loved her from the first moment and was gloriously happy when Grandpa said she was mine, all mine. Can you imagine such a moment? I spent time with her every day, getting acquainted, leading her around, teaching her from the beginning because I wanted to start winning some Barrel Races. She's been the best for several years. That is, until a rider named Shannon Wilson joined the competition." Jill laughed. "I should kill you for taking my dreams away. Instead, I think I'll just fall in love with you."

Shannon laughed. "I must say I'm glad you've changed your mind. You and Cameo have been fantastic. I've been training Pinto with you in mind. We're up against the best; win or lose, I just want you, Cameo, Pinto and I to decide to be together for years to come."

"Honey, I'll compete my damndest around the barrels, but never in the relationship I think we can enjoy."

They talked until well after midnight then went inside to the shower where they joined with kisses and loving under the warm water. From there, they enjoyed sensual pleasures under the sheets.

The following morning, Shannon went to her room to change clothes, pack her things and move into Jill's room.

After ordering breakfast in the hotel cafeteria, Shannon said, "I'm counting on you and I being mean competitors in the arena. Pinto and I are going to do our best to win this year and I hope you and Cameo do the same. Let's give the crowd something to get excited about."

Jill sipped her coffee. "My thoughts exactly. I don't want anyone to say we're doing any less. Cameo and Pinto deserve the best from us. Win or lose, I think we both have already won."

"Yes, something far better than a Dodge truck, especially when we'll be sharing the prize after the competition is over. Next year, we'll try to win a second one. Then you can have the older one." She laughed.

"Maybe we'll draw straws to see who gets the new one." Jill crossed her fingers then waved them at Shannon. "I'll win then."

They laughed and continued their conversation while eating breakfast.

At the rodeo grounds, Shannon and Jill spent most of their time together.

When the final night came, and the final barrel racing challenge was over, Shannon and Pinto had won the Dodge truck. Jill and Cameo were just two points behind them.

The following day, after loading their horses, Jill pulled her truck and trailer with Cameo inside, over to Shannon's truck. "I'm sure you can find your way to my ranch, just twenty-six miles north of Vegas. Even so, let's stay close. Just follow me."

Shannon laughed. "Honey, I'll follow you anywhere."

They arrived at The Cameo, Jill's ranch, before dark, put the horses in the corral, fed them then went inside.

Jill opened two cans of beer for them, then they sat on the patio under the elm tree to talk about their recent days and wins before going to bed together. There, they shared sensual moments and love's passion before going to sleep.

The next morning, Jill cooked breakfast while Shannon sat at the table with a cup of coffee. "I love your ranch. The location just below the purple mountains is perfect. My grandfather's already ninety-one and tells me he's giving the farm to me when he's gone. Gramma died four years ago. It's in Idaho. I'm the oldest grandchild but I'm not a farmer. My brother's the farmer. I hope Grandpa gives it to the two of us instead. If he does, I plan to sell my half to my brother. My life will always be Pinto and Barrel Racing."

Jill set the food on the table and sat down. "Shannon, I know I want us to stay together, to always be together. This ranch can be ours together. I hope you're thinking the same way I am. I know I'm already head over heels in love with you." She leaned over to share a kiss.

"Me too, with you, Jill. I've watched you from afar, and that was wonderful. But now, Hon, I love you. I'd want to be with you even if neither of us owned property or champion mounts. The four of us belong together. I'm loving you more every hour."

Jill, Shannon, Cameo and Pinto spent the year together and continued to train and practice barrel racing while their love knit their hearts together.

They still live on the small ranch twenty-six miles north of Las Vegas.

Love on the Farm

Maude Oliver lived a two-acre farm where she had chickens, a pet turkey, two horses, a cottontail rabbit and two sweet little dogs. Only the chickens had both a positive and negative purpose for Maude. They laid eggs most days, and occasionally, one of them provided Sunday dinner for her and her friends.

Living alone for the last six months had been hard for Maude. When her sweet Martha died, her heart was broken and her home was an empty place to be. Even so, she kept herself busy doing all the housework needed and tending her lawn, but not Martha's garden.

One day she determined to deal with Martha's garden so she grabbed her hoe and went to the untended garden. She stopped to look over the various vegetables, saw the turnips and beets were overrun by the weeds, not her favorite things to have in her garden. She took the hoe handle in both hands, bent her back and began to dig out the weeds.

Hours later, she had finished digging the weeds by the roots, raking them into a pile and throwing them over the fence, so the City would remove them the next time they came through to pick up trash.

She went to the shed where she opened the shed holding riding gear, saddles, bridles and other items for the horses. She smiled as she patted Martha's saddle. "I miss you so much, my sweet Martha. Every time I've come out here with the intention of taking Red and Honey for a ride, I turn into a crazy bunch of tears. Maybe today I can keep my composure and take them out for a while. I miss you so much." Maude's tears rained down, as they had done since the cancer took Martha from her.

Determined to follow through with her plans, she picked up Red's blanket and bridle. Then she whistled for the horses. Red made a long whinny, flipped her head back then ran toward Martha. Honey followed then ran ahead.

She tossed the blanket on Red's back and put the bridle on her. "Honey, you can trail along with us today. Your Honey, my sweet Martha's not with us now." She led both horses to the shed and put the saddle on Red.

With Honey in tow, she rode Red down the driveway to the road and headed toward the abandoned school ground a quarter of a mile away. As normal, there were no cars on the rural road so they had a pleasant ride. At the school ground, Maude let the horses graze on the tall grass at the south end of what had once been the children's play area.

While they grazed, Maude remembered her early school days in Moore School where no more than fifty students sat at the desks for first through eighth graders. She laughed as she remembered the day of the first snowfall when most of the students enjoyed a snowball fight. The two teachers didn't enjoy the fight as much so they punished all involved students.

"Would you believe, Red, I was one of twenty-two students who got a paddling; that's a whipping with a board by the meanest teacher." She laughed. "All the others wrote a hundred times, 'I will not throw snowballs at school.' The paddling didn't hurt; and we still laugh about that day when any of us get together. Martha liked that story and she had a few of her own to tell about her escapades at her rural school."

****

Through the late forties and early fifties, rural Oklahoma students attended the two-room schoolhouses before being bused to high school which was a much larger school with many more students. Maude Oliver and Martha Sims were talented enough to qualify for the varsity basketball team.

Maude, a brunette with blue eyes, had a slender figure and in school, she was the most talented player on the basketball team. She was also the pitcher for the high school women's softball team. A pretty girl with an infectious smile, she had many friends wherever she was. She was one of those girls whom the boys liked as if she was a good sister who could always be counted on for advice and friendship.

Of all the friends in her life, only one was dear to her heart, only Martha.

Martha was tall, with dark blonde hair and green eyes. A beautiful young woman, she wore the newest fashions and her hair was always in the most popular style. The boys in school, and wherever she went, admired Martha and flirted with her. To them, she looked like a Hollywood actress growing up in Paoli. She knew their intentions but had no interest in them; her heart belonged to her friend, Maude.

After graduation, Maude and Martha both went to the teacher's college in Oklahoma City where they shared the same dormitory room. They were together day and night except when in separate classes and their relationship developed into something more than 'just friends.'

Their romantic hearts didn't seek boyfriends or another girl as a 'best friend' because their romantic hearts were drawn only to each other.

It was after they returned from Christmas with their families that Maude and Martha had their first serious talk about the feelings of their hearts.

That day, Martha returned from taking a shower and preparing for bed then she stood for a moment just looking at Maude who was lying on her bed reading her Sociology book. She smiled as she felt warm, special feelings around her heart.

Maude looked up at Martha while closing her book. "Let's talk. I'm wondering about something." She moved to the far side of her bed and waited for Martha to sit beside her.

Martha hung her towel on a chair then sat on the bed. "And, my friend, what have you been wondering about? Maybe I'm wondering about the same thing." She smiled.

Maude fingered the blanket, looking at what her hands were doing. "You and I have never dated. In high school where the boys were always flirting with you, Martha, you didn't date any of them. You and I just played sports and with each other. I always wanted to be with you. You were special to me those years."

"You were just as special to me. Nobody else made me any happier than you did; not even Wayne Pearson whom I thought would never quit trying to win my heart."

Martha laughed. "He's probably still disappointed. But I just wanted to be with you."

Maude smiled. "I know. I was at the library yesterday and came across something interesting. The more I read about what was called Dorothy's Sewing Circle about Hollywood actresses, the more I thought about you and how I feel about you, Martha. Have you ever read about it?"

"No, but you've got my curiosity thermometer raising real high. What's it about?" Martha lay on her stomach with her feet in the air. She looked up at Maude. "Tell me about it."

Their room was small with twin beds and a chest of drawers which they shared, two drawers for each girl. It had two small electric lamps on the table between the headboards; each girl controlled her own lamp. Two windows let the daylight in during the day, but darkness closed in fast during the short winter days in Oklahoma City.

Maude lay on her stomach with her feet up and her face resting on her hand. "Hollywood actresses who loved each other would meet at Dorothy's Sewing Circle to be with other women who loved women instead of men. They had parties as a group, and no men were included in their relationships.

"Martha, some women love women and those who do, find ways to be together with the one they love. I think we're like those women in Dorothy's Sewing Circle. I know I don't think I could ever care as much about anyone else, man or woman, as I care about you."

Maude looked down and began to pick at a thread on the bedspread. She didn't know how Martha might accept what she was saying, nor what it meant for the rest of her life.

Martha brushed one fingernail across the other, scraping red nail polish off. After moments of silence, she looked up and saw tears in Maude's eyes. "I know I can't imagine being as close to anyone as I am you. They say we love our family, our friends and a special someone because of the messages our hearts give us. We don't think about the feelings, we just accept them and enjoy being close to whom our hearts tell us.

"Maude, my friend forever, you mean more to me than any other person ever will. Sometimes I daydream of you and I living together somewhere in rural Oklahoma and we work at different places so nobody knows who we live with. We love each other with the same closeness I've seen between my parents. I guess that's my dream for my future, to be with you every day in our home together. That sounds like a special kind of love to me."

Wrinkles crossed her forehead as Martha added, "It also is something people in general, would not approve of."

Maude nodded. "I know. And, I know what my heart tells me. I never want to be with anyone else but you. Right now, I want to hold your hand and be real close to you. Martha, can I kiss you the way I feel right now."

Martha moved close to Maude put a hand on her shoulder and moved toward her until their lips touched. A soft slow kiss was shared followed by smiles.

"Thank you. Your gentle sweet kiss gave me chill bumps all over. Martha, I love you."

"I love you, Maude; I really do." Martha moved in for another kiss.

Maude wrapped both arms around Martha and pulled her close. The two college women knew they were sharing romantic love with each other. Their hearts melded into one of romantic love, a love that must be kept secret.

It was 1955 in their Oklahoma dorm room that evening, the two college co-eds decided to always be together regardless of the challenges society offered.

****

Martha died in 1975 at the age of fifty-four.

Maude continued teaching high school English and Grammar, while she enjoyed working the two-acre farm. At her age, she never expected to meet another woman with whom to share her life.

By 1975, society had become more and more aware of homosexuals in their midst. Such people who loved the same gender were never understood by heterosexuals who considered themselves normal and anyone else ugly and abnormal. There was intolerance in every facet of life. Homosexuals had been considered criminals, especially the men who loved men. Women loving women were more easily accepted and their close relationships questioned less than the men's.

During the same years, there was a significant amount of publicity about homosexuals in San Francisco and New York City. In 1978, Harvey Milk, an openly homosexual man elected to political office in San Francisco, was murdered along with the mayor and others by an anti-homosexual fanatic. Prior to his death, Harvey Milk had led in parades and political rallies designed to secure acceptance of homosexuality.

Maude went about her life as a single woman. Society wouldn't consider her a widow, but she knew that was the right word to use. Her beloved Martha had died as they lived as wives so that meant she was a widow with an empty heart.

One Sunday at church she met a new friend, a woman her age who had begun to visit her church every Sunday.

A few weeks later she invited, Sara Quenten, to join her for "an old fashioned Sunday dinner."

Sara followed Maude home from church and parked her sedan behind Maude's car. Climbing out of her car, she smiled as she looked around. "Maude, you're got a whole little farm here. Horses, chickens and everything; how wonderful."

"Thanks, Sara. The horses love to be ridden. Do you ride?" Maude was pleased as she watched Sara's delight.

"I love to. I haven't ridden for years, but rode a lot at my grandfather's farm during my growing-up years." Sara followed Maude inside.

"We'll take a ride after dinner. Right now I need to change clothes, then I'll go kill a chicken for dinner. I've got a dozen fryers just right for the plucking." Martha laughed then went down the hall to change from her church outfit.

She put on jeans and a long-sleeved shirt, and returned to the living room. "Sara, would you like to change into more comfortable clothes? I have some that would fit you."

"Sounds great. I sure can't ride a horse in this skirt." She followed Maude to the second bedroom where Maude selected one of Martha's outfits for her to wear for the afternoon. "While you're getting dressed, I'll take care of the fryer." She went to the kitchen and put water on the stove to boil. It would be needed for removing feathers from the fryer chicken.

Maude smiled, and shook with excitement at having Sara visiting her. There was something special about her; and she liked wearing jeans and riding horses.

She went into the pen where the young chickens were getting fat for Sunday dinner, caught one and took it to a grassy area outside the pen. Taking the chicken's head in her right hand, Maude shook it fast, twisting the neck until the body flew off the twisted neck and landed several feet away. She moved away from the dead chicken and watched the body flip and jump up and over, around and around, until the muscle response to losing its head caused the fryer chicken to lay dead.

Before she went inside to get the bucket of boiling water, Maude saw Sara watching her from the doorway. As she approached the door, she said, "I didn't plan on you seeing that. It's the way my grandmother killed chickens; she'd just twist their necks like that. Then we kids would clown around with the dead chicken, daring the poor thing to jump at us."

"My grandmother did it the same way. I remembered how my brother and I acted when the de-headed chicken flopped around, like yours did. It was fun back then." Sara laughed and held the door for Maude to carry the boiling water out to the waiting dead chicken.

While Maude dunked the chicken into the boiling water to loosen the feathers, Sara stood nearby talking about life on her grandparents' farm. "I feel right at home with you, Maude. I love your way of life. I have so many memories flooding my mind right now. Being here brings me joy."

When all the feathers were removed, Maude used the gas blower to singe the tiny pin feathers off of the chicken. After that, she butchered the chicken, cut it into pieces, then to the frying pan. While it fried, she made mashed potatoes, poke-salad greens and corn-on-the-cob.

Sara smiled when she sat down for dinner. "Maude, this is wonderful. Everything you've cooked is on my favorites list. I'm so glad you invited me today."

After dinner, the two women went to the shed, saddled Red and Honey and went for a ride up the hill to the area where the abandoned schoolhouse once stood. Garvin County had closed all the rural schools and bussed students to the central school in Paoli, the same school where Maude and Martha had played basketball and softball. They went back to church that evening, then went to their separate homes for their work week.

Having dinner together became Maude and Sara's regular Sunday afternoon. When Maude didn't cook dinner, they ate in town, then went to her little farm to ride the horses. The more they were together, the closer their relationship became.

The Christmas season came and Sara went to spend Christmas Eve with Maude. She took her clothing so she could spend the night and all Christmas day. Christmas morning, Maude prepared a normal breakfast with eggs, bacon and homemade biscuits with hot coffee. Sara tore a biscuit in two parts and added butter to them. "Maude, you're a wonderful cook. I'd love it if I could have a breakfast like this every morning. It's all delicious."

Maude liked what she heard Sara say.

She had begun to have deep, loving feelings about Sara, and wished there was some way, someday, to ask her to move in, to find out if she shared the same sweet feelings when they were together. "Thanks, Sara. There's a room down the hall if you're ready to move in. It's yours anytime." She smiled.

Sara smiled and looked into Maude's face. "I really mean it, Maude. Do you? I care for you, very much. When you've mentioned your Martha, I've wished I could take her place."

Maude was stunned and happy at the same time. She had seldom spoken about Martha out of fear that Sara might be offended if she knew they loved each other exclusively. She hadn't realized that what little she said about Martha had communicated their love; and now, Sara was speaking as if she had similar feelings from her heart.

Maude stopped eating and looked into Sara's eyes. "Are you saying you care enough about me to live with me? You know what other people will think. They'll think we are a couple who love each other. It's not as easy to keep a relationship secret now as it was when Martha and I graduated from college."

"I know. Yes, Maude, my heart is drawn to you. May I move in and care for you the rest of my life. I know my feelings are of love, love for you. I don't care what other people think. I'd like to be with you day in and day out. If they no longer want us at church, that's their problem. Yes, Maude, I love you."

Tears filled Maude's eyes. "I'm so happy. I've been in love with you, and wished for this. Sara, I love you." She stood to hug Sara.

Sara stood up and fell into Maude's arms. From the long hug, the two lovers kissed and hugged some more.

Maude helped Sara move into her home that week and they began their lives as lovers; even as they knew, there might be troubling times as the word of their relationship got around the community.

They might be terminated from their jobs, chased out of their church, cut off by Sara's family, have their house burned down or other serious happenings from people who would hate them. Even so, they chose to be together in love for the remainder of their lives.

God's Peace...True Love

Sitting beside the lake where she and Amelia had met, Mary Jane Oltman remembered their years together. Falling in love was her most wonderful experience.

If she had been home that night, could she have prevented what happened? Why couldn't Amelia be sitting at her side, looking over her shoulder as she did that day twelve years ago? So many questions.

Mary Jane focused on the lake to find inspiration in the beauty her eyes could see; even so, her mind seethed with anger at the loss and hatred that had stolen love from her.

With her canvas on her knees, Mary Jane chose green chalk and began to draw the skyline where the trees met the sky. Her tears blurred the scene and she could no longer sketch what her eyes viewed. Instead, she scribbled her anger onto the canvas; first with the green, then with black, brown and red chalk.

She had come to create the serenity of the lake and the leaves shimmering in the distance; instead, she was lost in the memory as her tears turned the chalk drawing to a colored mass.

"Oh, God, help me. Please take this sadness, this anger, from my soul. I need to find peace, not distortion, in my life. How can I put Amelia's death into some perspective? God, help me find my way."

She tossed the canvas into the lake, fell on her face, and cried as her insides tightened with physical pain as though her heart was tearing to pieces.

Exhausted, she lay still, then went to sleep.

****

Her dreams took her to a place of light where pastel colors of light danced around her. Gradually, the scene around her came into view. She was not alone.

Women surrounded her and ministered comfort to her breaking heart.. They caressed her long blond curls, hummed soft melodies, gave her bread to eat and water to drink. Streams of light pierced her being to bring tranquility and peace.

After a while, when she felt overwhelmed with the peace they offered, the women walked away.

Mary Jane heard footsteps behind her. When she looked around, she saw Amelia, smiling and reaching her arm to touch her shoulder.

She felt joy flow through her body as Amelia sat beside her, enfolded her in loving arms and drew her close.

"My dear, sweet Mary Jane, rest in my love and find God's gentle peace. The reasons I had to leave will be understood by you one day. The love we shared still fills you, surrounds you, and will bring certain blessings for the remainder of your days in life. I did not want to leave you, but there was a higher purpose taking place.

"Know, my love, you will find blessings and the purpose. Know also, I will always be right beside you no matter where you are or what

happens in the years you have ahead of you. Some day we'll be in a truly beautiful place together until the end of time."

Mary Jane smiled. "I'll always love you, Amelia, always." She snuggled like a child in her mother's arms, into Amelia's embrace.

****

When she awakened by the lake, she sat quietly and closed her eyes to remember what she had experienced. Was it a dream, she asked herself, or was it real?

The physical pain and the scribbled canvas were gone.

After a while, she went to her car and got a clean canvas, then returned to sit by the lake again. She began to draw, not the lake and the trees, but soft colors of lights and the women who ministered peace to her heart. In the center of the canvas, she sketched the scene with Amelia and wrote the words, "God's Peace".

That evening at home, she sat looking at the canvas, trying to understand the words she heard from Amelia. What did she mean by "higher purpose" causing her death? How could anything of value come from the hatred that led to her death?

Mary Jane was confused yet remained at peace.

Her thoughts went to that terribly sad day.

****

Mary Jane had driven to the nearby grocery store. While she was gone, Amelia fed their two little dogs, put steaks on the barbecue and potatoes in the oven for their evening meal. She did not see the three hoodlums, men dressed in black, who crept to the front door and threw military grenades into the house. When Maude returned, she found the road closed by police. After she identified herself, a police officer informed her that her house no longer existed.

Their home had been blown to shreds. Mary Jane was left alone.

Police eventually arrested the three men who had murdered Amelia and they were sentenced to life in prison without the possibility of parole. They were members of the same religious faction, 'skinheads' who bombed the home of a lesbian couple in Salem in 1992 when voters declined same-sex marriage.   The religious fanatics and white supremacists hated homosexuals and were angry enough to kill innocent people using Bible references to prove they were on 'God's side.'

****

Healing from the loss of her beloved Amelia, Mary Jane used the life insurance money to establish a special "Amelia Foundation for a Higher Purpose" designated to seek civil rights for gay Americans. Thousands of donations were sent to the Foundation by Americans of every state. The words Amelia had shared with Mary Jane in her ethereal, spiritual experience, "a higher purpose" became the motto for the Foundation and her life.

During the following years, Mary Jane joined with others who were determined that homosexuals, people whose romantic hearts love their own gender, share the same rights as all other Americans.

Armed with purpose from Amelia's words and the power of their love, Mary Jane became a fluent speaker who helped lead the changes, not only for marriage but for all civil rights of her beloved gay community. Amelia's love for her was the power behind her actions and words.

Late one day, she had adjourned the February meeting of the Amelia Foundation, and was leaving the auditorium when she heard someone call her name.

She turned around and saw a woman her age, hurrying toward her. Waiting for her to approach, Mary Jane smiled. She looked into the bright emerald eyes. "Yes, can I help you?" She felt drawn to the woman, almost magically, as she waited for a response.

"Mary Jane, I'm Keri Brownlee. I want to buy you a cup of coffee or glass of wine just so I can get to know you. Will you join me?" She smiled. Her dark hair curled around her face and below her ears on which she wore tiny cuckoo clocks, delightful earrings.

Freckles across her nose were beauty marks on perfect complexion while her red lipstick gave Mary Jane a thought about how nice it would be to kiss such perfect lips; it was the first time she had such desire since losing Amelia.

Mary Jane smiled at her interest in kissing Keri Brownlee. "Yes, Keri, I would like to join you. Where shall we go?" For a moment, Mary Jane felt Amelia's presence and enjoyed thoughts of her.

"Well, the Pink Dragon is just down the street. We could walk there." Keri took Mary Jane's hand in hers.

Mary Jane looked at their hands, smiled, and started walking with Keri.

They walked toward the Pink Dragon, Portland's lesbian bar.

 The street was well-lighted and a slight sprinkle of Portland's rain fell on them but neither of the women seemed to notice. Each was feeling a warmth of happiness within her heart.

The two new friends had many things to talk about. Amelia's story and the Foundation were central to their discussion. After Mary Jane liked Keri; there was something warm and wonderful about her.

"Mary Jane, Edith and I were together eight years until cancer got her just over a year ago. I'm doing okay now, but it took some time to get over the grief. She was a teacher in Ontario, Oregon, while we lived across the Snake River in Idaho."

"Sorry for your loss; it's so hard to bear for a while. I'm so glad we're sitting here together tonight." Mary Jane took Keri's hand in hers as she sipped from her glass.

The two new friends shared conversation and laughter until late in the evening then walked to their cars. After making a date for the following Friday, each drove to her home.

Friday evening, Mary Jane wore her pale blue pant suit, a bright blue blouse, pearl necklace and earrings; and when she looked in the mirror, she smiled. "Woman, you look great tonight. I'm glad you've been smiling so much these recent days." She laughed at herself for speaking aloud.

Keri arrived at Mary Jane's house wearing a white dress jacket, dark slacks and a white blouse with ruffles down the front. Before she could get out of her car and knock on the door, Mary Jane came toward the car. When she got inside, Keri kissed her.

They went in the Pink Dragon where a live band provided music for the dancing lesbians in the ballroom. They danced together most of the evening then went into the bar to sit at a small cocktail table where they could talk for a while without the loudness of the music.

"Keri, holding you close and dancing tonight has been wonderful. It's my first date since Amelia's death. I'm so glad we're together." Mary Jane took Keri's hand in both of hers. "You're so beautiful, not just your lovely face but the kind of person you are. I love how you care about all types of people, not just the sometimes 'odd' ones in our gay family, but everyone you meet." Mary Jane leaned in for a kiss.

"As do you, dear woman. This has been a great evening. I'm counting on more." Keri smiled.

"There'll be more, Keri. I was thinking of a place I want to take you. Tomorrow, I'd like to drive you to Chesterfield Lake. It's a beautiful place." Mary Jane sipped her Coke.

Later, Keri drove Mary Jane home, then went to hers. The following morning, Mary Jane drove them to the lake.

They sat together on a boulder to enjoy the serenity of the place. Mary Jane sipped from her bottle of Coca Cola. "Keri, I'm falling in love with you."

"And I with you, Mary Jane. Wonderful feelings are flowing through me. I love you." Keri kissed Mary Jane and held her close.

"Keri, the last time I was here, something amazing happened. It was unreal and changed me.

"I came to sketch the serenity of the lake, the trees, and the whole scene. But, all the pain of losing Amelia and the ugliness of those who killed her tore at me. I fell apart." Mary Jane looked down at her hands and picked at a fingernail. "I cried so hard and went to sleep. Then I found myself in an amazingly beautiful place, quiet women were like angels ministering to me. Then Amelia was there holding me, and encouraging me.

"I still don't understand what happened, but God answered my prayer for help to get past the power of the loss." Mary Jane paused, looked into Keri's eyes. "It was all so real that day."

Weeks later after many dates, Mary Jane hugged and kissed Keri. Then she looked into her eyes to say what was on her mind. "Hon, I don't know how long we're expected to wait but I want us to marry and spend every day loving each other more and more."

"Sweet woman, whom I'll always love, the only rules are our own. Let's go across the Columbia River this week and get married." Keri smiled.

"Let's do. And, let's find a home in Vancouver so we can have all the civil rights available in the State of Washington. I love you so much.

They hugged and kissed then Mary Jane looked across the lake. "What a peaceful place to share our faith and our love."

"Until the sundown of our days." Keri smiled.

Ann Patterson

Interlude at Alcatraz

Marlene joined a San Francisco group for a day trip to Alcatraz Island, formerly a federal penitentiary. Most of the group was women Marlene's age.

She expected a sunny day on the island and had worn her straw hat with a red ribbon blowing in the wind, white Bermuda shorts and a red top. Her long, wavy blond hair blew in tandem with the long ribbons of her hat. She had a great smile that easily drew people to her for friendly conversations.

From the time the boat was loaded on the bay, she had her eyes on a certain someone. Trusting her 'gaydar,' she made her way to the gorgeous redhead standing near the barrier, looking back at the City. She stopped close enough for their elbows to touch; then the redhead who was wearing baby blue shorts and a pink blouse with a nicely low neckline, spoke. "Hi again. I saw you back at the ticket station. How're you doing?"

"Hi. I'm Sonja. Are you 'family'?" She smiled and Marlene knew which 'family' she meant.

"Oh, yes. I just knew my gaydar was right on. I'm Marlene. Let's walk a bit; get away from the crowd." Marlene smiled as Sonja took her by the hand.

They followed the crowd off the boat and into the big doors of the ancient federal penitentiary. The stone walls were foreboding. Marlene thought about how foreboding it must have been for the convicts, America's worst, were delivered there in chains and handcuffs. The hallway was dark.

Marlene shivered. "It would have been horrible to spend years and years here. The cells are so small, and who could appreciate having an open commode so close to their pillow. Yuk!"

Sonja laughed. "I think they said something worse than 'yuk' while in there. Remember, they were the worst among criminals and never expected to leave Alcatraz."

Tour guides led the crowd down, down, down into the tiniest cells where nobody wanted to spend time, in the "hole" so dark, so fearful to the touring crowd.

"Let's go back to the boat and have a smoke," suggested Marlene. "Nothing's here except ugliness. I'd rather be looking at you, Sonja. Your hair's beautiful, as are your eyes."

"I'm with you. I don't need to see anything else. I'd rather just be with you." Sonja put her arm around Marlene's shoulder and they turned back to the stone stairs and hurried outside.

Many other people had done the same thing so there was quite a crowd waiting to get back on the boar.

The Captain blocked the gate that would take them to the boat. "I'm sorry folks. We've had a problem with the motor. This boat won't be taking you back. I've radioed back to base and they're sending another boat but don't know how soon it will be here. It shouldn't be too long.

We'll sound the horn three times when it arrives. I'm sorry but we didn't foresee the problem."

Grumblings rumbled through the crowd.

Marlene didn't grumble; she had a plan. Most of the crowd moved against the wall of Alcatraz to wait for the boat.

She led Sonja toward a trail, which she knew from an earlier trip went down to the water, a nice private place to share with her new friend.

"The water seems so fearsome around the island. It's easy to see why nobody ever really escaped. If they got out of the building, the water was ready to drown them. I like to go down near the water and listen to the crashing waves."

"Me too." Sonja followed Marlene down the path then they turned toward a tree that grew beside the concrete wall up and higher than the barricade where Sonja had been standing earlier.

She glanced at Marlene and liked the smile she saw and the way her eyes twinkled.

Marlene stopped under the tree, looked up and saw that nobody above could see them from the barricade. She sat down without turning loose of Sonja's hand. "This is nice."

As Sonja sat beside her, Marlene put her arm around Sonja's shoulders.

To her surprise, Sonja cuddled close to her then turned her face with a smile. "I'm glad you led me here. I've hoped we could get some private time on this trip."

Marlene smiled and looked into Sonja's eyes. "I've looked at you with more than my eyes. Of course, I don't know if you're with anyone, but I've wanted to be alone with you. And, here we are." She patted Sonja's shoulder.

Sonja looked into her eyes and grinned. "Oh, yes. I'm counting on the rescue boat being slow to come for the group." She put her hand to Marlene's cheek and began a kiss, slowly at first then the kiss became passionate.

For the next hour, Sonja and Marlene shared sensual passion with kissing and caressing lips, face, breasts and special hidden places. They were in no hurry to enjoy the excitement of sensual, sexual loving until each of them swooned in her passion as gentle massage and kissing thrilled her from head to toe.

Eventually, the Captain of the boat blasted the horn three times, then three times again.

Weak in the knees and high on passion, Sonja and Marlene returned to the boat; only two guys got there later than they did.

Marlene tapped Sonja with her elbow, then nodded toward the two guys. "Betcha they had a good time too. "They're definitely family. My gaydar's blazing."

When the boat docked at its port, the new lovers walked together to Marlene's car.

Sonja stopped to make a suggestion, "Let's go to the Rainbow for a drink. I can't say good-bye here. Can there be more for us?"

Marlene laughed. "I hope so. Hop in, I'll drive. We'll get your car later."

Sonja got in the car with Marlene. "Thanks. Even if we're never together again, I know I can never forget our interlude on the island.

"Who said bad things happen at Alcatraz?" Marlene grinned.

After the Cloudburst

Sally hurried from her car to get to Anna's Dress Shop before it closed; she made it inside just as the owner was heading to lock the door.

"I made it. I had to get here before you locked up. I need my party dress that's on layaway. It's not too late, I hope." She brushed her bangs from her eyes; running had messed with her strawberry blond curls.

"No, my customers are always on time." Anna Benzow smiled as she reached to take Sally's layaway slip. "I'll have it for you in a moment." She hurried to the back room.

Sally took her wallet and comb from her purse then began to comb her hair. She was glad Anna had mirrors everywhere. Looking closely in the mirror on the desk, Sally saw a pimple in that same place, right in the center of her chin. "Darn it." Gently, she popped it then took facial make-up from her purse and covered the red spot. Then she smiled and checked to be sure she had no lipstick on her teeth.

Anna returned with a box. "That will be $26.00, and it's all yours."

Sally handed Anna her credit card, picked up the box and was prepared to leave as soon as Anna gave her card back to her.

Anna followed Sally to the door. "Watch out for rain. It looks like we're in for one of Portland's sudden showers; you know how it pours when that happens. Be safe." She locked the door after Sally rushed through.

Sally hated that she had to park a block away. The first raindrops fell on her head; they were the usual huge raindrops that preceded a downpour. "Darn it." Sally started running, then the heel of her shoe broke. "Double darn it! Not now! No!"

She bent down to pull off both shoes because it was impossible to run with only one high heel in place.

The cloud burst. The rain poured in streams.

Anna ducked under the only overhang nearby, hoping not to get any wetter than she already was. "I hate these cloudbursts."

A voice behind her said, "Me too; they come at the most inconvenient time."

Surprised that she wasn't alone, Sally looked around. Her heart skipped a beat. She saw the most beautiful woman with long black hair and perfect features who looked like the gorgeous Elizabeth Taylor; in fact, she started to say, "Elizabeth Taylor" but caught herself. "Hi" was all she could muster.

"Glad you've joined me. I was just heading to the Rainbow for a drink; now I'm drenched."

"I'm Eliz...I mean, I'm Sally Benzow. I'm going there later. They've got an 'all girls' dance scheduled for tonight."

Sally felt a bit silly for almost saying her own name was Elizabeth Taylor. She hadn't noticed she had said the wrong last name.

"I'm Meg Martin. Maybe this particular cloudburst is a dream come true." She giggled then pushed herself as far back from the pouring rain as she could get in the small space. "There's not much room here, but enough for us to share until it stops. I didn't know there'd be a dance tonight."

"Yes, I just picked up my party dress. Now that you know, will you be going?" Sally looked into Meg's blue eyes and smiled; she loved dark hair with blue eyes, so much brighter than her golden eyes and reddish blond hair.

"I don't know. I'm not dressed for it, and since I'll be taking the bus home, I may not go back out if it keeps raining." Meg had intended to have a drink at the Rainbow then go home for the evening.

She didn't own a car yet;. She was new in Portland and didn't trust using the bus services in late evening.

Sally shivered. The cloudburst hadn't let up. "I hope this stops soon. I'm cold."

The temperature always drops quickly during a cloudburst; afterwards the temp usually gets warm just as quickly in Portland, Oregon.

Meg removed her jacket and put it over Sally's shoulders. "My sweater's keeping me warm enough. You need this more than I do."

"Thank you. I haven't seen you at the Rainbow. I usually go by after work, but have had to work late for the past week."

"That's why you haven't seen me; yesterday's Happy Hour was my first time there." She put her hand around Sally's shoulder to keep the jacket from slipping off.

Sally cuddled closer to Meg. Grateful for her generosity, she thought how nice it would be to turn her face toward the kissable lips now near to her ear.

The cloudburst stopped as quickly as it had begun.

"Meg, can I give you a ride; it will save you from standing at the curb for the bus and getting splashed by the cars or the bus."

"I live in the St. Johns area. That's too far for you to take me but we could ride together to the Rainbow." Meg didn't want to take advantage of a 'good Samaritan' but she did want to be with Sally longer.

Sally looked into the blues again. "You're in luck. I'm not far from the St. Johns area. I'll drive you there or the Rainbow. I just want to get out of these wet clothes and get a different pair of shoes before the dance." She smiled.

"Then we'll travel together."

Sally took Meg's hand and hobbled barefooted to her car. "Can you drive? I don't have a decent pair of shoes on."

"Be glad to." Meg waited for Sally to unlock the car and get in then she hurried to the driver's side.

While she drove toward the St. Johns Bridge, the sun reappeared and created a glare on the windshield. She put her sunglasses on. "Sally, since we both want to go to the dance, why don't we stop at my house first, so I can change for the Rainbow and the dance. Would that be okay?"

Sally smiled. "Sounds perfect."

Meg stopped the car in front of a small house surrounded with flowers and a white picket fence. "Sally, why don't you bring your party dress in and get dressed here? I might even have a pair of shoes that will fit you; if not, we can go get yours."

Sally grabbed the box and followed Meg to the door.

Once inside, Meg went to the kitchen and put two cups of water in the microwave for tea. "A spot of tea will get us warm."

Sally followed Meg down the hall.

In the bedroom, Meg turned around and smiled as Sally removed the jacket.

"Meg, you got really wet after giving me your jacket. Aren't you cold?"

She liked the way Meg's blouse clung to her skin, showing tensed nipples. A twinge rushed through her thighs. She liked the feeling and wished to taste those lovely nipples.

Meg saw Sally looking at her. She smiled and slowly unbuttoned the blouse. "I'm as horny as a cat on a hot tin roof this very moment with you. Let's share."

She watched Sally's eyes move toward the happy nipples, and grinned.

Sally smiled and raised her shirt over her head, tossed it away as Meg's lips were on hers.

She shivered, not from the cold but the sexy woman's breasts touching her own.

Slacks and panties fell to the floor as the passion-filled women fell to the bed, ravishing each other with lips, fingers and legs. Their naked thighs quickly were wet, not from the cloudburst but 'cuntburst'.

Wild desire consumed both women.

Sally's hungry body heated up with every touch and kiss. Tingly sensations swept from her smiling face to the tips of her toes. She wanted more and more of that wonderful excitement.

She could tell Meg was equally as her body wriggled and pushed into Sally's face, demanding increased sucking and tension.

Fingers, lips, tongues played constantly as the women's bodies electrified and burned. Passion inflamed every nerve and hungry desire.

Then, in the same sudden climax, Sally pushed her mound against Meg's face, and Sally did the same, wanting Meg's touch to be deeper and faster.

Steaming bodies clung together and then relaxed.

With big smiles, they kissed and lay face to face with their legs wound together.

Sally smiled and looked into Meg's blue eyes. "Thank God, for the rain."

"And thank you." Meg smiled and kissed Sally. "We're hot and the tea's cold." She laughed.

Sally laughed. "And I'm not ready to cool down. It's crazy that I just remembered, I said my last name wrong. I had just been in to see Anna Benzow, and was so taken by your beauty, that I said her name instead of mine. I'm Sally Benson, not Benzow." She laughed again.

"That's the funniest thing I've ever heard. I've never done it. It's even funnier that you remembered it this minute. Sally, I was hungry for you instantly." Meg kissed her long and slow. Her hands began to caress the beautiful breasts she couldn't resist.

Sally hands gently caressed Meg's hair. "Eventually, we'll have tea."

Meg smiled.

Twenty Years to Love

The twentieth year class reunion of Westside High School's Class of 1967 was underway at the Red Lion Ballroom, Norman, Oklahoma. Agatha Picardy went into the ballroom, said hello to a few former classmates whose faces or name tags indicated their names. She saw an open seat and walked to the table. "Is this seat taken?"

Nancy Lehman, whom she recognized, nodded and waved her hand toward the seat, suggesting she sit down. "Nancy, you look great."

"Thanks, Aggie. Life's been good to me." Nancy was elected Student Body Treasurer when they were seniors.

Louise Mackman was sitting across the table. "Aggie, you look wonderful. Where have you been all these years? I've missed you at every reunion." She hurried around the table to share a hug. "It's great to see you."

After the hug, Agatha explained, "I've never been stationed near enough to come to previous reunions. I'm here now and, Lou, I'm so glad you're here. We've got a lot to catch up on."

She said hello to Nancy's husband and the others at the table.

The servers delivered plates of food and filled the glasses for the group at the table who laughed and talked through dinner. Agatha and Louise raised their voices as they talked across the table. The music and chatter of the crowd made it hard to hear each other.

Agatha cut her catfish steak. "Lou, what are you doing now? I've retired from the Navy and just moved back to Norman. I've been many places around the world these twenty years. Most of the time, I've worked as a clerk, so nothing dangerous; just interesting."

"I'm proud of you, Aggie. Thank you for serving. Our military needs good people like you. Thanks. As for me, I've had the same basic job with Clark and Clark Law Firm. No excitement or travel, just ho-hum living here in Norman."

Agatha spread butter on her bread roll. "I just took the job as Executive Director for Children's Futures here in Norman so I'm home to stay. And, I'm still single. Most of the women who joined the Navy twenty years ago met their man and left the service. As usual, I didn't follow the crowd. What about you? I don't see a ring there."

She pointed to Louise's left hand.

Louise laughed. "There are too many divorces in our generation. I've stayed single. Haven't found someone I've wanted to spend the rest of my life with. End of story, at least so far."

Agatha looked across the table into Louise's indigo blue eyes. She felt strong wonderful feelings pass through her heart.

She was anxious to see Louise after the event ended.

Louise contained her excitement at having Agatha there. At earlier reunions, she missed Agatha but having her across the table that evening was exciting.

A band began to play. Agatha excused herself from the table to roam from table to table, making contact with a few friends.

When she returned to the table, there was an empty chair beside Louise. They talked a while then Louise picked her purse and the reunion packet, "Aggie, I'm ready to leave. If you don't have other plans, will you join me for a drink?"

"I'd love to." Agatha stood up and turned to Nancy. "Nancy, I'm so glad to have seen you tonight. I hope we can touch base now and then. I'll be looking for volunteers to work with disabled children. You'd be great with them." After similar messages to the others at the table, Agatha followed Louise to the door.

"Aggie, we can go in my car." They walked Louise's fancy Lexus sedan.

Before starting the car, Louise looked at Agatha. "Before we go, I need to tell you something. Aggie, I'm still single and have recently acknowledged to myself that I'm a lesbian. One of the reasons I know is that I've carried feelings for you since our sophomore year. You surprised me by being here tonight. If I've seemed anxious, that's why. Where shall we go?"

Agatha giggled. "Lou, this is uncanny. To find you at Nancy's table was perfect. Things really do happen for a reason. My first class reunion, and I leave with the single person I had hoped to see tonight. Shall we go to the Rainbow Room?"

"Sounds perfect. I go there often." Louise smiled then drove to the Rainbow Room, Norman's gay and lesbian bar.

After their drinks were served and the dance music began, Louise stood up. "Shall we dance?"

With a smile, Agatha took her hand then they held each other close for a slow dance.

They stayed on the dance floor through two more songs, a lively dance then a slow one. When the music ended, each was looking into the eyes of the other. They shared a sweet kiss then a wink and a smile.

"Aggie, you're a great dancer." Louise sipped from her drink then took Agatha's hand to her lips. "Having you here is so perfect. It's my life's dream."

At that moment, a friend of Louise's stopped at her table. "Hey, Lou. Who's your girlfriend? I thought you had a class reunion tonight."

"Hi, Megan. This is Agatha, she came to the reunion." She winks.

"Hi, Agatha. Lou, is this Aggie whom you've told us about?" Megan grinned as if she was being mischievous.

Agatha recognized the teasing Megan intended. "I'm the one. That's why we're here. We weren't ready to shock our classmates by dancing together at the reunion." She grinned.

"You got me on that, Aggie. All of Lou's friends have had their fingers crossed that you'd come." With her hands, Megan made a joke about their fingers being paralyzed due to being crossed for good luck. "It's so good to meet you. You guys have fun tonight."

Agatha looked at Louise. "You've got some good friends, Lou. I thought I came on my on volition, but it must have been because of those crossed fingers." She took Louise by the hand and they laughed together. "I'm glad I'm here right now, with you. Let's dance."

Agatha led Louise to the dance floor, held her cheek to cheek and glided across the floor. She smiled as she remembered high school days when she had a crush on Louise but didn't fully understand what it meant.

Tonight, she knew. Her heart was warm as her love for Louise cruised through it.

Agatha kissed Louise's cheek and whispered. "I've missed you through the years. Now, I'm so happy, Lou. I had a crush on you all through high school and it never went away. You're why I'm still single." Their slow dancing continued through three songs.

When they sat down, other friends of Louise came to their table to meet Agatha before they left the dance.

At closing time, they went to the car, enjoyed a long hug and kiss, then Louise asked, "Shall we go get your car? Aggie, I hope you'll come home with me. I just can't say goodnight."

"We can get my car later. It's parked in a good place. I want to be with you tonight, Lou. We've missed too many years already."

At Louise's home they sat in the kitchen with cups of hot spiced tea, relaxing and enjoying conversation about their lives. It was as though they wanted to know who each other had become over twenty years of life experiences, both good and bad. The more they knew about each other, the closer their hearts wound together.

Agatha kissed Louise. "Let's go to bed. Lou, I want to hold you close and tell you over and over again that I love you because I've loved you more than twenty years."

Lou led Aggie down the hall to her bedroom and turned down the bedspread. After a passionate kiss, they rolled to the center of the bed to share the love and passion stored in their hearts for over twenty years. With that kiss, the two women became lovers for the first time. They kissed, they touched, and they soaked in every touch of love that blessed their bodies and their hearts. Twenty years of loving melded their very souls in the next hour.

The July sunshine awakened Aggie at her usual early hour as if the alarm clock had buzzed. She lay quietly watching Lou sleep. Just as the years had begun to change her own face, she saw the same kinds of wrinkles around the eyes and mouth of the woman she had always loved. She wished they had been together while the changes had happened. Since that had not happened, Aggie promised in a whisper, "I'll never leave you again, Lou. If we could have been together then, I don't think I would have ever left. All that love I've carried through the past, I'll share during our future together."

Lou opened her eyes. "Thank you, Aggie. I hope you'll move in and let my home be yours. I hope your sweet face is the first face I see every morning for the rest of our lives." She pulled Aggie's lips to hers.

During the next weeks, Agatha moved her few things into Louise's home.

Louise changed the title to include Agatha as joint owner.

For Louise's birthday, Agatha decorated their home with "Happy Birthday" streamers and invited many friends to celebrate her "39th and holding" birthday. Everyone had a great time.

After the friends left, Louise hugged her lover-wife. "Aggie, I have something for you." She opened her hand to show Agatha the diamond ring that she wanted to put on her third finger, left hand.

Agatha smiled. "Oklahoma may not let us marry by law, but our marriage is in our hearts. I love you so much, Lou." They wrapped their arms tightly around each other not wanting to ever let go.

Louise and Agatha have shared love and life as a happily married couple in Norman, Oklahoma, more than twenty-five years.

They are just one couple among thousands awaiting the day when their state will allow them to legally marry.

ABOUT THE AUTHOR

Ann Gross Patterson, now living in Portland, Oregon was born in Pauls Valley, Oklahoma, graduated from Fresno State University, Fresno, California, and taught "Creative Writing" to eighth grade students in Ceres, California, starting in September 1960.

Like so many other writers, from her days of teaching "Creative Writing" in 1960, Ann intended to be a writer, often declaring the topic she thought her first book would cover. And, like others, she kept putting off the day to begin to write. Now, she encourages other people who consider they'll write some day, to begin at the moment; not put off until some day, but start now.

After writing hundreds of essays and short stories, Ann found her preferred genre, Lesbian Romance, as the result of her "coming out" as a lesbian at the age of sixty. Her Lesbian Romance collections called Lesbians Rock, addresses the stories of lesbians of all ages, in all walks of life, living somewhere in America. Her stories tell of teenage girls coming out to themselves and each other, and stories of women like her who followed the norm in society by marrying and having a family before acknowledging what they apparently knew all along, that their hearts were drawn romantically to women, never toward men.

The stories in this collection have been written from the heart of a woman who seeks to increase understanding and acceptance of gay individuals and couples, the lives they live, and the sweet, gentle love in their hearts. These stories carry the message that romantic hearts everywhere are really the same, and love is love, whether the heart is drawn to a person of the same or different gender.

Ann Patterson

Pride for Who I Am

At sixteen I knew my heart
The way it loved set me apart.

For romance and whom to choose,
My choice someone I would lose.

My sister's heart chose many a boy;
To me they were friends, like a silly toy.

My father told me he was always aware
Whom mine chose; it gave him great care.

He said I was a lesbian; must then be wise,
Telling a girl I loved her could be my demise.

He asked I keep it secret until much older
Then "come out" a day when strong and bolder.

I married the man who sought me four years,
Divorced in sixteen when he had me in tears.

Raised my three children as a single mother;
Focused on them and loved no other.

Waited 'til sixty to make a choice for me,
Came out as lesbian for all to hear and see.

Mother believed God would send me to hell.
Dear father was dead; him I could not tell.

My children hugged me, their love was so true;
"We're glad for you, Mom; don't ever be blue.

Pride filled my heart as I lived my true life,
Ignoring all people who caused me strife.

Joy and excitement have filled my heart
Pride leads my way, I'm no longer 'apart.'

I met dear Molly whose love came to me;
We're living as wives for all people to see.

Pride fills my life, no secrets are mine
While I live each day with love sublime.

Ann Patterson

Ann Patterson